T0158490

EBUR
UNDER THE NIGHT JASMINE

Born in Baramulla, Kashmir, MANAV KAUL has been an integral part of the film and theatre world, acting, directing and writing for the past twenty years. With each of his new plays, Manav has made people sit up and take notice, and he has created an equally valuable body of work as a writer. His books *Theek Tumhare Peeche* (Right Behind You) and *Prem Kabootar* (Love Pigeon) have been dominating the Nielsen bestseller list.

VAIBHAV SHARMA is a translator and poet from Saharanpur, Uttar Pradesh. He was the 2023 Hindi Translation mentee under the NCW Saroj Lal mentorship programme, mentored by International Booker Prize winning translator, Daisy Rockwell. His work has been published in Out Of Print, Words Without Borders, *Hans* and *Modern Poetry in Translation*. He was shortlisted for the Armory Square Prize for South Asian Literature in Translation, 2023. This is his debut book in translation. He is currently working on a translation of Anil Yadav's story collection, *Nagarvadhuein Akhbar Nahin Padhti*.

ALSO BY MANAV KAUL

Rooh
A Bird on My Windowsill

Under the Night Jasmine

Manav Kaul

Translated from the Hindi by
Vaibhav Sharma

EBURY
PRESS

An imprint of Penguin Random House

EBURY PRESS

USA | Canada | UK | Ireland | Australia
New Zealand | India | South Africa | China | Singapore

Ebury Press is part of the Penguin Random House group of companies
whose addresses can be found at global.penguinrandomhouse.com

Published by Penguin Random House India Pvt. Ltd
4th Floor, Capital Tower 1, MG Road,
Gurugram 122 002, Haryana, India

First published by Hind Yugm as *Antima* 2020
Published in Ebury Press by Penguin Random House India 2024

Copyright © Manav Kaul 2024
Translation © Vaibhav Sharma 2024

ISBN 9780143465560

Typeset in Adobe Garamond Pro by Manipal Technologies Limited, Manipal
Printed at

www.penguin.co.in

Preface

I used to dream of writing a novel. Whenever I was writing, and a story started to look and feel like a novel, my hands would shake violently. 'Are you a novel?' I kept asking the story. But the stories never had any interest in turning into novels. And so, they would stare back at me as though I were a criminal. I would neglect the stories as I pursued the scent of a novel. I wanted to quickly reach that part of the story where the scent first emerged. Like when you're walking down the road at night, and you catch a whiff of night jasmine, and suddenly you're taken by a keen desire to see the plant, if only once. I just wanted to hug that night jasmine once and tell it stories of how I was wasting away, waiting for my novel to arrive. Probably it was a mistake to think that I would achieve my goal by running after stories that looked and felt like novels. I wandered the deserted streets of those stories, but I never saw any night jasmine. After a while, the stories lost the fragrance of novels and sat down to protest right then and there. Innumerable stories have been lost in this quest. But I never gave up on my childish search.

For a long time, I blamed my inability to write a novel on my childishness and fickleness. Maybe that's why I wanted to grow old quickly. After a while, I didn't know what I was waiting for. The novel or old age? It's not possible to age quickly and eventually, I left my longing for a novel somewhere on the road of life. Last year, I was passing through some small European villages, working on my travelogue. I got so entangled in my travel writing, that whenever I caught a fresh whiff of the night jasmine, I thought it better to record it on paper rather than run after it, and thus, I postponed the search. I remember I was in the mountains when I was putting the finishing touches on my travelogue. In those days, everyone I met would ask me the same question, 'Can you smell that fragrance too?'

'What fragrance?' I would ask.

'Of night jasmine.'

I tried time and again but couldn't catch the scent while in the mountains. For a long time, I believed that my dissatisfied stories had somehow robbed me of my ability to smell night jasmine. I even wondered if I myself was the source, as everyone I met mentioned it to me. But I laughed off the thought, as a child too I fancied myself the Phantom.

After Europe, I was so busy with my personal life that I wasn't able to finish my story collection, though it wasn't for the lack of trying. *Chalta Phirta Pret* wandered around me like a ghoul. All of a sudden the coronavirus came and everything froze in time. To me, it felt like a huge scientific experiment was being performed and all of us were the lab rats, asked to stay indoors. For days I thought about the rats that are used in lab tests. After a few days of disbelief, I understood how important this time was. How important it was for us to stop and let this blue planet breathe; it has tolerated so many human cruelties without being allowed a single sigh of discomfort. All of us quickly accepted the lockdown because it was like growing old together; nobody was alone in this.

For a homebody writer like me, this time was no less than a boon. I hovered over what I had written. Soon, I finished my story collection and sent it off to my editor, Shailesh Bharatwasi. The story collection got stuck within the constraints of the lockdown but my work was done and hence I had lots of time on my hands. My editor said to me, 'If you have any ideas, write them down.'

My editor pushes me ever so slightly and so simply to write the next thing that sometimes I don't know if I'm writing something of my own free will or merely at his encouragement. 'I don't feel like writing anything right now,' I said to avoid further discussion. But what he said got stuck in my head. I remembered that this time last year I had been wandering around European villages. I never imagined that exactly one year after my European tour, I would be locked up in my house against my will. I was raring to go on a trip again. I looked through the photos from my travels the previous year, turning the pages of my travelogue *Bahut Door Kitna Door Hota Hai*. That's when I smelled the night jasmine again. After so long I could sense it was close. I thought if I reached out, I would be able to touch it. Like it was somewhere nearby. It might have been at an arm's length but I was unable to touch it. So I opened a fresh document and started writing in a bid to put out the fire burning in the jungle tinder that was my heart. 'There was night jasmine somewhere in this very jungle'—this was the sentence where the story was supposed to start but I didn't write it down. I didn't want to get bound by anything. I wanted to record the fragrance, free of all restrictions.

'I knew a failed writer by the name of Rohit'—I started the story with this sentence but didn't write this one either. I turned it into a seed and sowed it in the desiccated jungle inside me.

I think expectation is an enigma concealed in the envelope of life. I'm very good at waiting because I'm always more interested in the envelope, rather than what's inside. Like a silent viewer, I watched Rohit crumble and fall apart for a long time. Then, suddenly, I felt that I could smell a familiar fragrance. I had been waiting for this for years. Not exactly of night jasmine, but something close to it. Just then I felt like someone called my name: 'Antima'. When I turned I saw a green sapling in the dry jungle, its name was Antima. This novel is an account of me wandering around that night jasmine and its scent, and the long stretches of repose in its shade.

I want to write a novel about silence.
The things people don't say.

—**Virginia Woolf**

1

A peculiar fear used to haunt me, the fear of spending myself. I'm not a miserly person and this had nothing to do with money. I was instead worried about spending myself. Always on the lookout to save myself, constantly worried about saving my quarter of the rupee. My mother came up with this rupee analogy years ago. 'Son, all of us have one rupee to spend in our lifetime,' she would say. 'How you spend it forms the basis of the life you'll lead. The first quarter is to be distributed among family and friends, and the next two are to be squandered away in the pursuit of a secure future, but you must hold onto the remaining quarter. It's for you and you alone. Don't spend it on anyone else, keep it for yourself.' While my mother was still alive, I never understood what she meant. Maybe she was trying to tell me something about herself, I thought; but then one day I accompanied some friends to see a play called Inshallah, and there I heard my mother's exact words spoken aloud on stage. If my mother were alive, I thought, I would tell her about this play, which somehow contained her words. That was the moment I decided that I'd never let my quarter of the rupee be spent; I'd hold onto it and keep it safe.

It's only now that I'm beginning to realize that we must spend most of ourselves; only then can we save a little. In the struggle between spending and saving, there comes a point where it's hard to discern which side we're on. In the aftermath, we sit holding onto that saved quarter and wonder what to do with it now that we have it. That thing we saved our whole life now stands before us, its gaping mouth a dark, infinite void. If what remains of us is actually infinite, then we have barely grazed the surface. Will it ever be possible to enter the inaccessible places inside us and open the doors we fought our whole lives to keep closed? Or will we die of exhaustion, waiting for those doors to open? This is the infinite, the unending. Until now, I only wrote what spilt through those doors, but today I decided I'd cross the threshold.

I take my remaining quarter and toss it in the air to spend on myself. A door opens. I step into the unknown, to places I've never been, places I've kept hidden somewhere inside me.

Inside, it's midday. Outside, a bird chirps. Inside, old songs traipse about, half-forgotten memories held within them, and I see the bird outside. No, it wasn't outside, not really, instead, it sat on the parapet dividing the outside from the inside. Its gaze shifted between the two. Outside there was the blue, open sky, whereas inside hung a cage. Outside lay the fear of freedom, inside, the ennui of safety. The bird hungered for flight, but its food lay inside the cage.

Every morning I wake up to the realization that this is not a dream. The entire human race is in lockdown; this is really happening to us. All our plans are turning to dust right before our eyes.

In the early days, there was the excitement of being a part of something historic, which, for the first time, was happening to the whole world at once. Like a trashy alien invasion movie. But now this enthusiasm was dissipating. What was left was redundant news and boring conversations, with everyone proposing their theories as to what the future holds. In all this uncertainty, it was difficult to believe our own thoughts. A temptation arose with endless free time to write, wasn't this what I've been waiting for? But I couldn't gather the confidence required to write in these astonishing times. And without that, what you write is lacklustre. I have words . . . a lot of them actually, and they look great typed up on my computer. I even get the aura of the story right, but there's that one lie in the story that makes so much noise in my head, that unless I delete everything, I can't sleep. So, I decided to spend these days doing nothing, just laying low and biding my time. I thought when everything gets back to normal, I'd go on a long trip and write. It looks like that's not going to be possible anytime soon.

My name is Rohit and I've been living in Mumbai for the last twenty years. I'm a script consultant by profession, but now and then I also write dialogues to make ends meet. When I left my village, I was excited to do many things, but as the years went by, I saw that excitement disappear bit by bit. The endless wait for that day when I'd write for myself has eclipsed everything else. In a feeble attempt to overcome my failures, I recently sent a manuscript of short stories to my publisher. Twenty years ago, I published two poetry collections titled *Tragedy* and *Blank Days*. But by the time those two were out, I had grown to hate poetry, and there were many reasons behind that. I could easily write a book on it. A thought: why not write about the days when I felt the first blossoms of poetry bloom inside me? Whenever I thought about those days a shiver ran down my spine. Although I've crossed the threshold, I still don't dare open some doors. My editor wanted me to compose another poetry collection, but I sent him stories instead. The lockdown has delayed publication. My editor is eager to publish the new book as soon as possible, he thinks it's important that people have a constant supply of books to read in these trying times and it's his responsibility to make new books available.

Is it impossible to bring the story, the struggles of writing it and the writing process together in a single narrative? The whole account of it, without any edits or cuts. I've always thought of the writing process as a whole world in itself, where characters can roam around of their own free will. For me, this process is as interesting as the story. Whenever I'm writing a story, I describe the process within it as well, but before sending it to the editor I remove that part. Who will be interested in such things anyway?

Sometimes I think that all of us have been sentenced by nature to be imprisoned by our memories. With or without someone, stuck inside our homes, all alone. This has had a bizarre effect. Can we write about this? All of us hide the pain of this imprisonment in our conversations. Because it's not exactly pain, and it's not exactly a prison. We're stuck inside our homes, while the world, in all its beauty, lies outside. We can't reach out to touch it, can't wander around as we desire. We've collected our freedom and wrapped it around our bodies, like clothing. But then we realized we didn't have much clothing to wear at home. We had never imagined we would need so much. Until now, we had slept in our work clothes only. Moved about in our homes in work attire too. We were never at home, even when we were physically present. We only stepped in to rest here, between going out, returning and preparing to return. And in these hours of rest too, we kept looking at the clock, the calendar, trying to gauge our future. Now this habit is making us lose sleep. What time is it? What date is it? What day? Everything has lost its meaning.

This May heat has me drenched in sweat. Taking a shower is postponed because I haven't made lunch yet. In my laziness, I always end up making khichdi. I opened the fridge and looked at all the vegetables, not because I wanted to use any of them but just because the cold air felt good on my face. Later, I made khichdi but didn't feel like eating it. So, I made some chai and brought it to the window with some toast. Everything had lost its meaning. Heat . . . sweat . . . and the chorus of birds. Last night, I woke up at ten past three. It's strange, but since the day I sent the stories to my editor, I've been waking up at ten past three every night. I wake up, take a look at the clock, drink some water and go back to sleep. But last night it took me a long time to return to sleep.

In the beginning, many of my friends used to call. We would laugh at the absurdity of this time on group video calls. Then all the jokes fizzled out and everyone accepted it as it was. Now we only talk occasionally, and that too feels like the labour we do to keep ourselves entertained. In any case, nobody has anything to say. The news is of the migrant labourers returning to their villages—crossing thousands of kilometres on foot, or bicycles—carrying their kids on their shoulders. These images have agitated me to my core. When I talk to my friends about this, we pick a villain in the end and shirk responsibility. But what else can we do?

We do whatever we can, but a sense of helplessness is always there and the anger it causes plays a constant role in our conversations. After saying everything we can, we change the topic to avoid the awkward silence. I tried to write many times at different points in the day but couldn't write anything in the face of the migrant crisis. So, I postponed writing for a while.

2

Keeping oneself busy is an uncomfortable burden. We see the day passing by and yet can't do anything to save it. I can't read any one book for long. For the past few days, I've been carrying a couple of books back and forth from the living room to the bedroom. Most of these books are old, books I've read. New stories seem to be getting lost somewhere inside me. It's similar to when someone calls me for the first time; I'm unable to talk to them for long. I always wish they'd say whatever it is they wanted to, quickly, so that I can disconnect the phone. But every time I rebuke myself for not talking to them properly, I must admit it's not like I have something more important to do. During these closed-off days, I want to take a leap of faith. I want to talk about the things that we keep away from our stories. Things which we edit out of our books just before printing them. Can we write about such things?

Today I started cleaning the house like crazy. I thought if everything was clean and vacant, only then would it be possible for something new to enter. Even if it's just more dust. I don't mind anything as long as it's new. After cleaning the house, I went to my bookshelf. While I was cleaning, I found so many old books there, books I didn't know I still owned. Stendhal, Turgenev, Mayakovsky . . . I had bought all these books in my early writing days from a Raduga Publishers stall. Russian literature was available for very low prices back then. I used to think it must not be any good since it's so cheap. But I wanted to keep books in my house to make an impression on girls and other friends. I would put these Russian books at the back so that nobody could see them; in the front, I'd display the authors everyone knew about. In the early days of writing, Russian literature helped keep me sane, but I still hid it from others, as though it were a shameful friend. Only later did I learn the importance of these authors. The corrupt friend turned out to be a true one. I still feel guilty about that. That's why I can't get myself to give these books away, even though I've given away so many others. These were my mates when loneliness stalked me, and I didn't know what to do. Gorky's *Mother*, Pelageya Nilovna . . . the name still gives me shivers. I touched and held those books for a long time. Every old book has some association. Just then I saw Camus' *The Outsider,* her last letter peeping out. A fine smell of cinnamon hit me the moment I opened that letter. In it, there's a Jorge Luis Borges poem called 'You Learn'. I got scared and shoved the letter back inside the book and hid it under a pile of thick books. A bead of sweat had rolled from my forehead to my cheek.

I turned on my laptop and sat down to write. 'You Learn' kept running through my mind. I tried to gather all my memories and write something down on the blank screen:

What time was it? What day? As time passed, the date and hour entered my memories too and started to mock me. I found myself standing in front of a dilapidated closed door! Should I open it? Should I enter? Just to know what time it was on that side of the door? What years of memories crouched there? The door creaked open, and I found Rohit from tenth standard sitting there.

He was reading a poem, 'You Learn'. I took a deep breath and the door snapped shut. The story had opened its eyes when I fell asleep. When I woke up that night to go to the washroom, I felt as if somebody was standing behind me, but when I turned and switched the lights on, there was no one. I looked at the clock and it was ten past three . . . again? As I drank my coffee, I kept thinking about the figure I had seen just before I switched on the lights. It felt like it was her. When morning comes, you laugh at your fears of the night, but each one of them returns to your side when the night falls again. Turn to the wrong side and you'll be face to face with them.

I read Antima's messages on my phone again and again. I was happy when she came to Mumbai for a few days for her company's work. We met over dinner. I had no idea that meeting her after all these years would make me so happy. She was in a relationship with some guy in Delhi, which I was happy about. After discussing the old days and much laughter and fun, I dropped her at her friend's house, where she was staying. Just before parting ways I had clicked a picture of us which she asked me not to upload on social media: *He wouldn't like the fact that I met you.* We were always better as friends than as a couple. Even today the amount of love between us comes from the time spent together. I looked at her for a long time and she apologized. I told her I understood, but actually I didn't. Why lie? She texted me a few days later and I got to know that she was stuck in Mumbai because of the lockdown and the friend she was staying with had moved in with her boyfriend. After I had a friend of mine deliver some rations and necessary items to her place, she said that she wanted to meet me. She texted multiple times but something didn't feel right to me, so I didn't reply. I wanted to write to her and tell her that I didn't want to meet her on the sly, but if we had talked about these things, we would have ended up ruining the memories of our time spent together, so I stayed away from my phone.

I had no idea when I fell asleep. When I woke up, I saw a lizard entering through the door. What time was it? What day? I shrugged the thought away. I was drenched in sweat. I got up and took a bath. A message alert pinged on my phone. I looked at it. It was Antima, writing that a friend of hers had brought her a bottle of scotch and she wished to have a drink with me that evening. She knew I could see the texts. The only thing I could do at this point was to block her, but the moment I did, our past would turn bitter. Every relationship is burdened by its most beautiful moments. We are willing to do anything to safeguard those moments. And so, we end up carrying the weight of that person on our shoulders, fearing they might step on our lived reality and walk away. Antima texted again: *You don't want to see me?* The bitterness in her words was palpable. I couldn't ignore her any longer. I replied: *Not today, maybe tomorrow, not feeling good.* She instantly sent a smiley back and said: *Okay, take care, see you tomorrow.*

I tossed the phone away.

3

I try to walk outside for an hour or so every evening and play music on my earphones, my eyes glued to the ground. Now and then, my eyes would wander off to the sky, shining brighter than ever before. I feel the slow pace of the evening affecting my walk every day. My body constantly moves forward, but my brain knows we aren't going anywhere, just walking around in circles. The flow of thoughts, while circling the same spot, feels soothing to me. Sometimes my eyes wander off to other people's masked faces, searching for hints of familiarity; almost all of them look the same. If you smile at someone or raise a hand in salutation, it becomes a responsibility. Now something will keep bothering you every day until you carry out the ritual with that particular person. All your thoughts stand still like statues as if the action is a trigger that frees one's thoughts. To escape these greetings and smiles, I either keep my eyes on the ground or stare at the sky. But how long can one escape?

Pawan, someone I had known for a long time, vowed to break through my facade. In the beginning, he would come and stand in front of me, so I'd have to smile at him. He'd greet me back with a smile and say something. When I pointed to my headphones, and thus couldn't hear anything, he'd walk away. Some days later he took to walking with me after our greetings. Whenever I looked at him, I got the feeling that I was the one who had invited him to join me. I tried to change the time of my walk, but it was either too sunny or too dark. I had to stick to my time. Then one day I thought I would tell Pawan that I wanted to walk alone. He was walking beside me. I took off my headphones and turned towards him. The moment I turned to him he said, 'I killed four lizards,' and hung his head.

'What? Why?' These words had escaped my mouth before I could stop myself.

'For many months there were these two lizards in my house, and I had no problem with them. You know how much I love animals.'

I wanted to say, I don't know. I don't even know you properly. But Pawan wasn't leaving any space for me to butt in, he kept talking, so I kept on walking and listening to him, hoping that whenever I get the chance, I would tell him, *bro, I don't want to listen to you.*

'Then one day I saw they'd had a baby. I thought okay, small family, happy family. Then I saw another baby lizard. Can you believe this . . . I mean they're in somebody's house and then they give birth to not one, not two . . . but four children. I mean, it's not fair, right? The lizard and her husband know where to go and where not to. But the babies! They're everywhere. It's not my job to teach them that this is milk and that is dal and that your place is in the corners of the walls! At least they shouldn't get into my bed. But I thought, they're kids, they'll learn. So, I would admonish them, teach them in my own way, but then yesterday afternoon, it got too much.'

He shook his head after saying this and fell silent for a while. This was my moment to get away, but if I left now, the 'too much' that had happened would keep nagging me and I wouldn't be able to write anything. It was more important for me to know the end of the lizard story. Pawan must have been in his early forties. His beard had grown out due to the lockdown, and most of the hair on his head had turned grey. I waited for him to say something but when he didn't, I had to ask, 'What happened next?'

He replied without looking at me, 'What to say . . . that afternoon I saw another lizard peeking in through the window and the two lizards in my house were staring back. I thought my house lizards would scare this outsider away. But then one of them went out and escorted the outsider in. That's when I understood their strategy. If someone is living with you for free, it's understandable, but if they take you for a fool, it can't be tolerated. I mean the lizards must have gone out and told the other one that the man inside is naïve, he's an idiot, so come in, stay, give birth to as many children as you want. The fool won't say anything; he'll even teach the young ones some manners. So, I picked up one of my slippers and killed the female first, then her three hatchlings . . . but when I went to kill the male, it turned to me and said . . .'

Pawan was silent again. I thought it was some trick to intrigue me. I was staring at him, but his face didn't betray anything, or it might have but I couldn't tell because of the mask. It couldn't be a trick, but how could he stop at such a cliffhanger? I was angry. I wanted to ask him how a lizard can speak. But instead, I said, 'What did the lizard say?'

'It said, "We trusted you." I mean obviously it didn't speak speak; lizards can't talk. But when you live with dogs, you talk to them as well. Someone looking in from the outside might wonder how someone could have a conversation with a dog, but only people who love dogs can understand that it's an actual conversation. Same way when the lizard turned and said, "We trusted you." My hands started shaking. Do you understand? We had a connection built over months . . . maybe years. We'd spent so many quiet hours looking at each other. They'd gotten rid of numerous bugs for me. But in the end, I turned out to be just another human being.'

Neither of us said anything after that; we just kept walking. I didn't put my headphones back on. Pawan was wearing slippers with his trousers and a shirt. I wanted to ask him why he wasn't wearing shoes. But asking that question would bring with it responsibility, and with the questions that would follow, a relationship will start to take shape, something which I've always tried to avoid. So, I stayed quiet. As he was leaving, he said, 'I've made brinjal today. Do you like brinjals?'

To that, I replied, 'Wah!' and walked away. My reply kept needling me for a long time, but what else could I have said?

4

I sat on my balcony till late into the night. There was a full moon. The stars looked bright and clear, but there was no breeze to speak of. Salim texted to ask for money. I said I'd transfer it tomorrow. Then I called my father and listened to him talk about his day for a long time. These days Salim stays with him all the time.

'If your mother was with us now,' said my father, 'she wouldn't have been able to tolerate all this staying in. Her feet were like wheels, just like yours.' I stayed up late wondering if having wheels for feet was the root of my problems.

'Why did you not sleep last night?' I asked my father.

'I did, but I woke up around three in the night. So, I just sat up in bed and waited for it to be morning.'

I felt like there was a deep quiet around me when I heard this, which contained the full moon and the stars but no air to speak of. In that quiet, I found myself standing in a corner of my father's bedroom as he sat in bed in the dark, staring at the walls. Sometimes I want to ask my father what he thought about in those silent moments. Did I think the same things when I stared at my ceiling fan for hours? Is it a genetic problem in our family to wake up around ten past three? After a certain age, we start to resemble our parents. We become a reflection of their habits, especially the ones we don't like. They sneak in and become a part of our daily routine. No matter how hard we try to shake them off, they come back again and again, till we accept them.

I tried really hard to not bring my father into my writing. But that's the problem with writing, you have to keep all the doors open and you have no control over who will enter and from where. If these were normal days, I could have stopped it from happening, but right then I was so wrapped up in my memories, I'd lost all control. My father was a part of my writing now and he would stay here with all his traits. How he would be a part of it was his business, as I don't like to talk to him that much. My father and I never got along well because I could never be that perfect child who could be shown off to the world to gain happiness. I had locked his happiness away years ago and that's why we often argued over the bitterness that remained in our house. When my mother was still there, she would intervene and sort things out. Now that there was no one to mediate, we had stopped arguing. As long as she was alive, she heard us bad-mouthing one another constantly. One day she got fed up and said that if all we had to say to her were nasty things about each other, then it's better if we don't talk to her. Our conversations with her shortened after that. After her death, we realized that there was so much we had wanted to say to her but couldn't.

I woke up again in the night. I didn't look at my watch this time. I was sure it must be ten past three. I sat up in bed.

Was my father sitting up in his bed like this as well? I had some water and lay down again. But then I got up again to pee. The light of the full moon shone so brightly through the windows, it was as if someone had turned on a tube light outside. I felt someone move behind me. I turned around to see a shadow move but when I turned the lights on, nobody was there. I didn't turn off the lights out of fear and went back to bed. But I couldn't sleep with the lights on either. So, I got up again, turned the light off and sat in the drawing room for some time. Who could it be? Do some fears never leave us, no matter how far ahead we are in life?

Light came in from the outside. There was a coolness in the air. The corners of the house were dark, but I could still see the entire room clearly. I lay down on the sofa but didn't dare close my eyes for a long time. Eventually, I fell asleep. Sometime later, I felt someone sit beside me. The sofa sagged a little near my head. I am a timid person, but I don't believe in ghosts and such. I am aware of the irony. I curse the irony, but there's no getting rid of it. I knew if I opened my eyes, there would be no one beside me. But with my eyes closed I could feel a presence. Then someone touched my hair. I lifted my hand to my head and touched the soft skin of another. I wanted to open my eyes, but I caressed the hand instead. There were no lines in the hand. My hands reached for her wrist, and I touched that thread which was still tied there. My hands stopped moving the second I touched it. I froze. A green thread. My heart raced and I held my breath as if I was hiding under water.

'Do you recognise me?'

I heard the voice and opened my eyes.

It was morning by then. Somebody was knocking on my door. I woke up drenched in sweat. It was the garbage collector. I gave him the trash. He complained about my doorbell not working. I checked and found that it was switched off. I apologized to him and turned it back on. He asked me if I bathed with my clothes on. I closed the door.

What time is it? Where am I? What date is it? Is everything imaginary? Was I asleep? Or have I imagined this life after being bored of my usual one? Or are we really going through a time when a disembodied voice talking to me on my sofa seems completely normal to me?

I thought about the hand all day, my mind stuck in the green thread and its fibres. The virus was spreading everywhere. News from all over the world came to me uninvited as I tried to shrug it off. I returned to my computer again and again, added lines and deleted several more. But this time the editing was different. This time I was removing things I would have kept in my writing on normal days. If everything around me was so abnormal, how could my writing stay normal?

At times, I felt like I was standing on a riverbank watching the water flow by. One day flowed into another like the current of a river. It was difficult to tell one day apart from the others. Because each day was the same. As I made tea, it felt as though I'd just made some, although it had been yesterday when I had. So, I made coffee instead and called my father. 'Son,' he replied . . . The sound of his voice gave me a sinking feeling. I didn't say anything for a minute. I could hear the music behind him. 'What songs are you listening to?' I asked although I knew very well what my father liked to listen to. I could hear him breathing, and after a while, he said, 'The evergreen hits of Rafi.'

'Did Salim cook you any breakfast?'

'He's making it now.'

'It's late.'

'Yes, he went out to get groceries.'

'Ask him to keep the vegetables in the sun for a while.'

He didn't say anything. Whenever he sensed me trying to care for him, he was alarmed. One time when Ma was still with us, during one of our fights he had said that he didn't want to be saved. *Don't tell me to walk, or what to eat, what not to eat, don't tell me what to do, I've no interest in staying alive.* We kept fighting over this until one day Ma was gone.

'What did you eat?'

'Nothing, I'm having coffee just now. I'll also play some Rafi songs.'

'Yes, enjoy.'

I know what makes him happy. It makes him happy to see me doing the things he loves. I for one was so tired of everything he loved in my childhood, that I couldn't tolerate them anymore. I was silent for a while before putting on a song by Rafi. When he heard that, he called out to Salim, asking him to talk to me.

'Salim, don't go out multiple times; just buy whatever you need in one trip.'

'Bhai ji, he loves fresh vegetables, but don't worry.'

I knew my father must be staring daggers at Salim. He didn't like it one bit that I controlled his life from here. When I asked him about my father's health, Salim went silent. I would have to call him separately; he wouldn't say anything in front of my father. Salim disconnected the call.

Where was I? The moment the call disconnected, I found myself in the village. Father was glaring at Salim and Salim was trying to reassure me. I saw my home. When did I get back here?

Silent eyes are different, they think more than they see.

A long text came from Antima. No guests were allowed in her building. She proposed to bring her friend's car to my compound, and we could then sit inside and drink. *Be ready at seven,* the text said. That meant she didn't want to hear any excuses. I texted back: *Tell your boyfriend you're coming to see me. See you!* But she didn't reply.

I'm standing in one place. The road to my destination is deserted. Every step I take feels pointless. But how long can you be stuck in one place? I start walking like I start writing. As soon as I reach the other place, the effort of it has comforted me. Small steps seem to me like small joys, which tend to linger for a long time. But if I stay in the other place too long, I'll be trapped in the dreams of the first. It's a tragedy to be stuck in dreams. I have no idea what's next for me in this journey, but whenever I've taken a step, something solid has given me a perch right before falling. When I resume my writing, I don't hesitate.

5

'Cheers!'

Antima had brought everything with her, glasses, scotch, ice . . . Her boredom made her do all this. She put on some of her favourite songs, and we sat in the car drinking. I was drinking scotch after a long time, so I finished the first drink fast. Just then Pawan texted: *Bro, won't you come for a walk today?* Antima saw the text too, 'You were saying you don't see anyone.'

'I go for a walk daily and this fellow has stuck himself to me; let it be.'

'Must be a friend, he has your number.'

'I used to go to watch his plays a long time ago. He does great theatre work, but we were never friends.'

'Do you have any friends at all?'

'What do you mean?'

'I mean is there someone whom you can call a friend?'

I had never thought about this. Whatever names I could come up with even after thinking long and hard were people who I barely talk to. I have friends, but not in the way Antima defines friendship.

'I have you!' I replied sheepishly.

'I'm not your friend; if I were, you would have asked me to meet you.'

'You know why I didn't want to meet you.'

'You're like a child. Your antics are laughable.'

I could see the shadows of our past relationship flit across her face. What a wonderful time we had spent together! We travelled to so many places. I turned my eyes away from her face. I shouldn't drink any more.

'How I handle my personal life is no business of yours,' she said while pouring another round.

'And I don't want to interfere at all.'

'So, it's my personal matter if I tell my boyfriend about meeting you or not. I want to see you and it's between you and me. You can certainly refuse to see me whenever you want, but you have no right to take any kind of moral stand in my personal affairs.'

I shook my head and sipped my drink. After some time, when she apologized, I just smiled at her. Compared to our present, our past has more of a hold on us. Although still inside the car, we had somehow moved back in time. She was looking much younger, and my perspective had changed. How long do we really live in the present moment? Is the present just a figment of our imagination and we're just shuttling between the past and the future? Antima spoke animatedly about her work, and I stared at a mole on her neck. It always seemed familiar to me. Could I reach out and touch it? I curled my fingers into a fist to control my hand. I didn't want her to know that I was looking at her mole. When she started pouring me another drink, I refused.

'Why not?'

'I haven't met anyone for a long time, and I don't think it's a good idea to drink more.'

Antima laughed out loud.

'You're so filmy!'

'Oh! so now I am both childish and filmy, thanks for the compliments.'

She used to say this earlier as well. I burst out laughing. Somebody knocked on the car window. It was the watchman.

'Sorry sir, but this is not allowed. You understand . . . please.'

'Arey, but we aren't allowed to bring anyone home. Can't we just sit here?'

'It is allowed . . . just ask madam to park her car outside and you can definitely take her home.'

'Okay.'

The watchman stood at a distance. We looked at each other and smiled. We knew that it wasn't a good idea to be alone at home after drinking as much as we had. I got out of the car. Antima poured another drink and handed it to me, 'Enjoy,' she said and left. I still felt the same pain now watching her leave as I did when I bid her farewell all those years ago. Back then she used to be Aru to me. I had never addressed her as Antima. Aru left and when she came back, she was Antima, a good friend.

6

In my tiring everyday life, I could feel something was about to unfold. However, I was unable to ascertain if that incident was going to happen in my real life or in the story that I was writing. I realized that I hadn't dreamt at night for many days now, nor had I woken up at ten past three. I had slept soundly for the past few nights, lost in a deep slumber. Even during the day, it was so easy to fall asleep. Sleep lurked in the shadows, waiting for my head to hit the pillow. Why was I sleeping so much? The entire house was in disarray. Chores had piled up. I hadn't even gone for one of my evening walks in many days. Pawan kept texting me, but I didn't reply. In one of his messages, he'd written that somebody wanted to meet me, and I should let him know if I'm going for a walk.

I was sick of Pawan. I couldn't meet anybody else. A friend of mine had said that sleeping a lot is a sign of depression. Was I depressed? Maybe I should ask someone who has gone through depression. But that's considered shameful and taboo in our country. Who would admit to being depressed?

I really needed to entertain myself and my only entertainment during this lockdown was the evening walk. I couldn't avoid it for long. I had just started when I heard Pawan coming from behind me.

'Arey yaar, why don't you stay near your phone? I texted you so many times. Did my messages not reach you? I thought my phone was malfunctioning! I thought since I'm not receiving replies to my text, I'll have to buy a new one.'

Pawan said the whole thing in a single go, and I was riddled with guilt. I should have replied to him. Pawan is a good man at heart. He just says whatever's on his mind.

'Actually, I've just been sleeping day and night.'

'Why?'

'I don't know. I think I'm depressed. That's why I couldn't reply to any of your texts.'

'Depressed!'

Pawan was quiet. I realized that I hadn't talked to my father in many days. I had transferred some money when Salim had asked me to. Suddenly, I felt like telling Pawan that I'd been unable to hold a conversation with anyone. I was not depressed, but I did feel a vast emptiness. I wanted to talk to my father, but I preferred it when we were both silent. I could listen to him breathe for hours on the phone but when he asked me, *how's everything going?* I had nothing to tell him. In the quest for a good conversation, all the affection drained away and a dreary weight was left behind. Sometimes I just wanted to call him up and tell him a joke. It had been a while since I'd heard him laugh.

Pawan motioned for me to stop and started talking to somebody on the phone. Oh, what had I gotten myself into? Pawan was not my friend. Why couldn't I tell him to take his call and I would leave? I used to go see his plays, but I saw other plays as well. I like theatre. Just because I watched a play shouldn't mean that I have to tolerate the playwright too.

I thought Pawan had left theatre. I neither knew what he did currently nor was I interested in knowing. I didn't want to take this friendship further than the walk. Pawan disconnected the call, and we resumed our walk. There was a spring in his step.

'Aru is a dear friend of mine, and she wants to meet you. That was her on the call; she will be here soon.'

Pawan had said this with complete authority. My heartbeat quickened after hearing that name. I wanted to refuse the meeting, but I couldn't speak. With a sad smile, I agreed to his proposition, though he did not care much either way.

'What does she do for a living?' I asked about Aru unwillingly.

'You can ask her when she comes. She's very dear to me.'

When a man introduces his female friend to another man but insists on words like 'dear', it means *I am introducing you to her, but I am in love with her so you must stay away*. I wanted to tell him that I wasn't going to hinder his love story, but as always, the time when I should have said it passed by.

'Have you ever thought about acting?'

I had to laugh at his question. He kept looking at me, waiting for a verbal answer.

'Never!'

'So, you came to Mumbai to write books?'

'No, I came to write films. But I was disillusioned after working in television for a few years. Now, I supervise scripts and write dialogue to make ends meet. I've been writing my own stuff for some time now.'

'Like what?'

'Stories?'

'For whom?'

'For myself.'

I wanted to add that I wanted to burn whatever I'd written, but I didn't.

'I want to try my hand at acting now. I've heard that there's a growing demand for people with salt and pepper hair. I met Aru in an acting workshop.'

'She's an actress?'

'She's an actress too.'

Whenever Pawan said Aru, I saw Antima and me, saying goodbye to each other at the Vienna airport. I tried to separate the two images. By then Pawan's Aru had arrived.

'Hello, I'm Aru,' she said directly to me. She put her hand forward to shake mine, but I replied with a namaste. I saw that her mask hung around her neck as well. She had a deep complexion and a beautiful smile. I was scared to see her, it was like my past stood in front of me. I lowered my eyes. After greeting me, she hugged Pawan, and we started walking together. The moment they hugged, my mind was filled with the virus and ways to avoid it. But I didn't say anything. The people who get attracted to you are like you and not like the person you want to be. For some unknown reason, whenever I meet someone new, such thoughts cross my mind at least once.

'Why don't you tell him why you wanted to meet him?' Pawan asked, breaking the silence.

'I've brought both of your books and I want to get them signed.'

She pulled both the books out of her bag and handed them to me. She was looking for a pen but couldn't find one. I was embarrassed to hold my books and was walking with my eyes on the ground. All the poems were full of guilt. A lie only I knew. I couldn't stand them near me for a long time. She found the pen. I just wanted to sign them and get out of there. As I was signing, she said, 'Please write something for me as well.'

'But I don't know you.'

'Write anything, just a few words,' interrupted Pawan.

'I've read both of your books many times and have gifted them to other people as well. I believe that if I wrote poetry, it would be somewhat like yours.'

Aru kept talking but I couldn't hear anything. I wrote whatever came to my mind. We kept walking and I was in limbo. A letter with the Borges' poem 'You Learn', stuffed inside a Camus book and thrown at the back of my shelf kept coming back to me. After some time, I interrupted Aru, made a shitty excuse and left. I didn't even look at her. Pawan shouted at my back that he would see me tomorrow. I turned back to smile. I was sure that I wouldn't be coming back for a walk.

I reached home and washed my hands. I had touched the books and the pen. I should be more alert. I was uncomfortably sweaty. Whenever someone praises my writing, I want to run and hide. I wished to reach a place where I couldn't hear or see anything.

I wanted to call my father and just hear him breathe. I took out my phone but didn't call him. I made myself a drink and came out to the balcony when my phone rang. It was an unknown number.

'Hello, this is Aru. I just met you with Pawan.'

'Yes?'

'Sorry for disturbing you. You must be writing, and I called you out of nowhere. Actually, I couldn't wait.'

'Tell me, what's the matter?' I felt agitated.

'Sorry! What you wrote in my books is very weird. At least I found it weird, so I thought I would call you.'

I had no memory of what I had written. Had I written something weird? Rude?

'Oh, did I write something wrong?'

'No, not wrong, you wrote that all the poems are a lie.'

We were silent for a while. I couldn't believe that I had really written that. I felt like I had been caught red-handed. I could barely get the words out when I spoke.

'I am so sorry. I will sign the books again, whenever I see you next.'

'I don't want to lose out on a chance to meet you again. You walk every day; tomorrow I will bring the books back.'

I was silent for a while, and then she disconnected the call.

I woke up at night. I checked the time: it was ten past three again. I sat up. There was a text on my phone, but I didn't check it. The light streaming in from outside illuminated parts of the room. I felt that I was asleep and dreaming about waking up in the middle of the night. I smiled and fell back on the bed. I had just closed my eyes when I felt like somebody was sleeping beside me. I shouldn't drink. I sat up again. The someone beside me sat up too. I left my bed and went to sit on the sofa in the drawing room. I saw someone standing by the kitchen. I could see the person clearly now. Straight shoulders, curly hair and a delicate wrist tied with a green thread.

'What are you doing here?'

Asking the question alleviated some of my fears.

The kitchen door moved a little and I couldn't see her anymore. If you sit your fears down and chat with them, you realize how pathetic they are. I knew what I was seeing. I went to the kitchen. Nobody was there. I opened my computer and sat down on the sofa. I pulled up a new Word document and stared at the white, stretching out before me. My breathing eased and I closed my eyes. A short while later she came and sat beside me. The secret and the fear were naked now. I slowly opened my eyes and started writing:

> **Verma Madam was his Hindi teacher in class 10. The terraces of his house and Verma Madam's house were a hop and a skip away.**

'You're lying again,' Verma Madam whispered in my ear. I knew she was sitting beside me. I had only written one sentence of the story and she could already sense the lies.

'It's not completely a lie.'

'A half-truth is as good as a lie.'

'You were my teacher. I was in the tenth standard. And whenever we met, we used to talk about literature.'

'But I taught you maths.'

'Which I hated.'

'I tutored you for free so that you would get more interested in the subject.'

'But we always just talked about literature.'

'Not literature . . . poems . . . poets.'
When her voice was gone, I resumed writing.

Their terraces were joined. For many days he was happy about the fact that a beautiful woman was his neighbour now. But when school was back in session, he realized that she was his teacher. One evening they were both on their terraces and struck up a conversation over the evening tea.

'No, it was over maths. I had asked some questions in class, and you kept staring at me,' Verma Madam whispered again.

'That's why I don't write for others, just to avoid such conversations.'

'I'm just stating facts.'

'Facts are boring, just like everyday life.'

'So our lived reality was boring?'

My gaze kept wandering to the green thread on her wrist. During these difficult days, when time and place had no value on their own, our past seemed to be just one step away from returning to us. You needed to take a small leap when you wanted to come back to the present.

'It wasn't boring at all.'

'Then why don't you write what really happened.'

'I want to write a story . . . a journey, like a free flight.'

'So does that mean you'll hide the Dargah, the deer, the swimming and the drowning?'

'I don't know.'

'You do too. If you aren't willing to write everything, then it's better to keep these doors shut. I won't let you fill up this house with your creative writing.'

'You know exactly where this story will end up if I start writing everything.'

'It will go to the person to whom it belongs.'

'I don't want to go there.'

'Near the fort, by the river side, under the peepal tree . . .'

'Shut up! I want to stay on this side of the river.'

'So, you want to write the easy stuff in these difficult times?'

'Yes, very simple . . . straight . . . normal.'

'Then write fairy tales. If you decide to write about the sunflower, you will have to record its death as well.'

'Does the writer not have the capability to change the past in his writing?'

'This is not that story. You can't escape telling it.'

'We'll see.'

'We'll see.'

I kept quiet. I closed my computer and realized that Verma Madam was no longer beside me. My legs shook and my lips quivered. I was murmuring something, I realized. With the rhythm of my shaking legs, Borges's poem 'You Learn' was spilling from my mouth. I was amazed at the fact that I still remembered it word for word.

7

The day was humid; there was a chance of rain. I had been staring at a murder of crows, busy with their lives, for a long time, when I heard some unfamiliar sounds. What bird was that? I had never heard that birdsong before. I followed the sound for a long time, but I saw no movement in the canopy of trees. I soon forgot about the bird and instead of the crows or the trees, I was now looking at the first rays of the sun. It looked like someone had been tossing gold dust all over the world. Suddenly, a yellow and rust-coloured bird appeared before me. It came close and hopped up and down as if inviting me to a game of hide-and-seek. Tiny, but complete in its beauty. The world around us is so beautiful and yet we know so little about it. Our blue planet hangs in this lone universe, revolving among all these other planets. We know nothing of the vast darkness, but we do believe that year upon year, the sun will keep rising and we'll continue to reach ever greater heights of success, as we plan for a future further and further away. And then one day, a virus borne by a bat stops the world in its tracks. How important was it for us to stop? We soon realize that all the dreams of the future were nothing but make-believe. The only truth is the beginning of a new day and with our interference gone, it's all the more beautiful. The bird hid itself again but this time I wasn't looking for it.

I called my father.

'Hello son, how are you?' My father answered the phone in a weary tone.

I know so little about my father's Kashmir, I thought. For a minute I stayed silent and listened to him breathe. I wished I could ask him if we could just stay like this for a moment, but I was the one who had called him; how much longer could I have stayed silent?

'Can you hear me?' he asked.

'Yes, very clearly.'

'You called so early in the morning.'

'I thought you must have woken up.'

'I didn't sleep at all last night, tossing and turning.'

I wanted to say, Me too, but I didn't.

'It seems like it might rain here today,' I said.

'Do you remember that road in Kashmir which had lines of trees on both sides?'

'Yes.'

'A Rafi song was filmed there.'

'Would that road still look the same?'

'Nothing has changed there. After everything is better, we'll go there and walk on that road, listening to that Rafi song,' his voice glowed with joy like a lightbulb about to burn out.

'Yes, have you talked to anyone there?'

He didn't answer my question and changed the topic. The lightbulb had gone out. I wasn't allowed to talk about Kashmir more than that. Now we were talking about everyday things and my mind wandered. Why did I not talk to Ma more when she was here? Now it's just my father, but no matter how hard I try to talk to him, there's a wall between us, impossible to penetrate. Whenever I went to see him, every step taken towards him seemed to make him more rigid. I feared if I came too close to him, he would go rigid like a dead body, and I would be the one left touching a cold corpse. I wasn't ready for that. Are we ever ready for death? I think it's the reason there's always a divide between us even when we meet. As if we speak in different languages, hail from different planets. Parents are troubled by their children growing up, the same way children are troubled by their parents ageing. But we don't say these things to each other, they're too silly . . . don't grow up, don't grow old. We just start avoiding one another.

'Listen to Rafi songs. Melancholy won't do you any good,' he said out of nowhere.

'Hmm.' I knew where he was going with this.

'And you should get married. What will you do after I'm gone? Who will you call?'

'Hmm.'

Like him, I too have my boundaries. And anyway, we've talked about these things in every possible way. Such conversations only led to quarrels, and after Ma, we both tried to avoid that. So, I kept quiet, and my father listened to my silence on the other end. Then he said, 'At least find a good job and stick to it. Buy a house; for how long do you plan to wander about from one rented house to another? You will get married once you buy a house.' I was amazed, after so many days, he was back to breaking his head on this wall.

'Everyone is stuck in their homes right now. There are no jobs. As soon as this is all over, there will be work.'

'I made Salim bring me your books. I am reading them slowly these days. That's why I asked you to listen to Rafi songs.'

'Why are you reading them? This Salim . . .'

I couldn't believe it. How could I tell him that it's not me in those poems? I knew he would read them and then comment on my loneliness and my love life. It was hard to explain to him that it was somebody else who writes them. I just endure it. He would try to decode me via every poem. How to stop him?

'There's a girl, Aru . . . she's very nice. I'll introduce you two some time.'

'Aru . . . that's a lovely name. Pass my blessings to her . . . I will wait for you to introduce us.'

'Ji.'

Afraid that I'd say something more embarrassing, I disconnected the call. I hung my head in shame and looked for the treachery of my actions on the floor.

When I checked my phone for the text, it was from Antima: *call me, it's important.* She had texted last night. I called her but she didn't pick up. I put on a playlist of Rafi songs and fell on the bed. A long time ago, Ma had sent me a photograph of my father. He was wearing his thick glasses and was rifling through the pages of my book. I immediately called her and made her swear on my life that she would take my books away from my father. She was frightened and took my books away from him, and as long as she was alive, my father never saw any of them. But Salim didn't have the courage to go into my father's den and take my books away from him. If it were possible, I would have gone to the village myself and burned those books. But everything seemed impossible in this lockdown.

Growing up, no matter what we were taught about becoming a successful person, the ultimate goal was to be rich and famous. Things learnt in one's childhood are of no use; with time, they fall like a house of cards and the illusion shatters. Anyone who thought as a child that they could get anything they wanted if they were stubborn enough, found it all come crashing down for them as they grew up. Their childhood looked like a sham to them. They were now a part of the world where the major issue was to survive. The person merely survives, but their aspirations are fame and wealth. There is no correlation whatsoever between what we learn our whole lives and what comes in handy at the end. Yet we want our kids to go through the same process. It's like we want to take revenge on the next generation so that they will have to go through the same ordeal as we did. But do people really grow up the same way? Everything is bound by the limits of possibility. Sometimes we reach so far out of our limitations that people are amazed, whereas at times some aspects of our being get stunted in childhood. Some people grow upward, others sideways, while some get stuck, despite their potential. And in all this, parts of our childhood crawl into our old age as well. We shuffle the deck of things we learnt in life, only for the king to laugh at us, or for us to pocket a joker and get back to work.

I used to cry a lot as a kid. Ma told me that I had had a sibling, but he or she had been stillborn. Did they hear me crying while still inside my mum and end their life out of fear? For many years, my father continued to remember that non-existent younger sibling of mine, saying that if he had been there, things would have been better. I was good at table tennis, but my father wanted me to be a swimmer. He would take me to the river with him and throw me into the water from the riverbank. People nearby would start shouting that the kid will drown, that it's enough . . . Only when I stopped thrashing around and started to sink into a state of unconsciousness, would my father fish me out. I'd had such a fear of water since childhood that I wouldn't bathe for days. But later I learnt to find coins at the bottom of the river. I came to love the underwater world more than the one above. If it were up to me, I would stay underwater forever.

I had just fallen asleep when Antima called.

'Hello, did you go to sleep early last night?'

'Yes.'

'Good, or I would have ruined your night.'

'You can attack my day if you want, it's not going that well anyway.'

'I'm not drunk enough for that now. Last night I had a lot of complaints from you, but now I just feel resigned about you.'

'Don't say that.'

'Sorry, I'm hungover from last night.'

We were silent for a while. I had nothing to say. And all she had for me was irritation. Then it was she who broke the silence.

'Can't we just meet like old times?'

'You know we can't.'

'No, I'm not talking about the lockdown.'

'Neither am I.'

'Listen, I want to travel with you, let's go somewhere.'

She knew how much I wanted to travel with her. I didn't say anything because I was too vulnerable.

'When we used to meet before, it felt like we were each other's happiness. I just want to experience that again. We used to meet for inane reasons . . . at any time of the day. We've run around in innumerable cities of innumerable countries. How can I tolerate being stuck in your city? You're twenty minutes away from me and we're unable to meet.'

'Maybe your boyfriend knows about this habit of yours. That's why you have to lie to him?'

Antima was quiet for a minute and then she hung up. I knew this silence. When we were breaking up, we would stay quiet on the phone to hide the intensity of our feelings. When you're madly in love with someone, you want to see them happy. We tried till the end to turn our deep love into a friendly affection. It's easier said than done, it takes years to achieve that, many painful years.

I felt bad for saying the thing about her boyfriend. Antima knew me. She knew I was trying hard to not see her. And I knew myself and my weaknesses. It wouldn't take much for me to break, so I had to maintain distance.

8

Nothing was changing outside. I woke up on silent mornings, ran around in circles during the endless afternoons, and then the evenings came to take away all the remaining energy from the house. Only nights brought relief amidst all this, pushing everything from outside into dreams. Once it was dark, it felt as if the entire day was part of a dream that would commence as soon as I fell asleep. The rest of the time, I roamed around the house like a wraith.

In the past few days, I had dreamt about Kashmir several times. I had thought I'd tell my father about the dreams, but he talked to me so little about Kashmir; what if it annoyed him? So, I kept my dreams to myself, away from my conversations with my father.

I never realized how much of my being was occupied with thoughts of Verma Madam. Only if you paid close attention would you know that this name constantly ran through me like a breath. What had happened, and what should be written down? I always felt that this choice rested solely in the hands of the writer. But in reality, he has no control. Trying to be honest with his characters is what pulls him down. Lies and treachery are easy in one's personal life, but the characters you create never forgive you. You have to go back to your story again and again, and it's only when you have taken out all the lies from your work that your characters let you inside their real selves. In the end, I had to keep my first meeting with Verma Madam in the classroom, where I was gawking at her and couldn't answer any of her questions.

In all this, Aru called many times, but I didn't pick up. I texted her to let her know that I was busy and would call her soon.

Aru had become a part of the lies I told my father. How could I bring myself to talk to her again? I'm very good at procrastinating. I believe that if I avoid some problems long enough, they'll end up solving themselves. I also ignored any messages I received from Pawan. I was frustrated with myself. Why do I keep pushing people away? Pawan is a good man at heart and a companion for the evening walk, but I always fear that this walk will soon turn into a responsibility, and once again, I'll run away from it and find myself a weak man, standing alone. I was bombarded with such thoughts. For how long would I live inside my own head? I was forever racked with guilt for others. I wanted to change myself. I wanted to apologize to everyone; Antima, Aru, Pawan, my father, Salim, Verma Madam. There was a self-serving motive behind this apology: because of this frustration and guilt, I was unable to proceed with Verma Madam's story. I needed her in order to write any further. There was no spontaneity in the story, and I was running out of the space inside me. I needed to do some cleaning.

First, I ordered two packets of Krack Jack biscuits to be delivered to my father at his home. They were prohibited for him due to diabetes. Then I called Salim and asked him to cook chicken for my father but hold back on the spices. I knew that this would make my father happy and maybe he would forget about Aru as well. Then I called Antima,

'Hello. Congratulations.'

'For what?'

'They're resuming flights starting next week.'

'Yes, I've already booked the tickets.'

'Great!'

'I'm sure you're happy.'

'Listen, do you want to go for a walk tonight?'

'A walk? At night?'

'It's too hot in the day, we won't be able to walk. We'll walk on the back road. Just like we did when we travelled.'

She was silent for a minute.

'Rohit, I'm very angry with you. I'll have to think about this.'

'Okay . . . I'll see you at the gate of my colony at nine.'

'Arey . . . I haven't decided yet.'

'I know you that much . . . see you.'

I said bye and disconnected the call. It was hard for me to watch her go. She knew this and I knew she would definitely come to meet me. It's so painful when someone leaves. Even if you don't have that deep connection with them anymore. Even a momentary connection, when broken, leads to the opening of a chest of memories and we realize that we've stored the last moments of all of our relationships like a film. We rarely remember the beginning of most relationships but there's immense drama in the final days, which we can't seem to get rid of. When Antima said she'd booked her return tickets, I wanted to go and meet her that very moment. I wanted to ask her to take a long trip with me. I wanted to give her so much love it would be impossible for her to leave for a long time.

9

That night I reached the gate of my colony around eight o'clock. I was cursing myself for behaving like this. I was doing the same things I always did. Why did I feel the most love for her right when she was about to leave? Aru called, but I didn't ignore her this time.

'Hello?'

'Namaste! I thought you wouldn't pick up this time either. Sorry, I hope I'm not disturbing you.'

'I should be the one apologizing. I was just a little busy. What are you doing tomorrow evening?'

Just then I saw Antima's car pulling up.

'Pawan is coming over tomorrow. He'll cook pasta. I'd be so pleased if you could join us too. My house is just a five-minute walk from yours. Please come, it would be lovely.' Aru was still talking, and Antima was signalling to ask me where to park her car. I guided her to the back. I walked up to her as she was parking.

'Okay, I'll think about it.'

'I'll text you my address. You can come any time after seven.'

'Okay.'

'Thank you! See you tomorrow.'

Tomorrow was far away, so I didn't worry too much about it. I was excited to see Antima. I looked at the time. Antima had arrived at nine-twenty. She was wearing jeans and a white T-shirt. She removed her mask when she saw me.

'Keep it on, we're going for a walk,' I said.

We were walking on the dark road behind my building. She looked beautiful today. I felt like I was looking at the old Antima. The road was vacant. Just some stray dogs roaming about in the pale light of the streetlamps. A police van passed by as well. The policemen saw us but moved on. Mumbai had never been this deserted. The city had started to look ill.

'I was reading some of your poems yesterday and couldn't stop myself from laughing. You've changed so much.'

'Why are you carrying my books around with you?'

'No, not the books Rohit; years ago when we had just met, you emailed me some of your poems. I just came across them.'

'In a bid to hide ourselves and mimic others, we end up writing lies, especially in poetry.'

'They are good poems, but it's not you in them.'

'That's the worst part.' I was flustered.

'But it's all fictional, and isn't all fiction a farce? Nobody's judging you for it.'

'But what about being honest to oneself? All that was driven by a need for validation.'

'But we all need some sort of validation. I like it when the emails I draft get more than a simple "approved" from my boss, sometimes a simple "good" would make my day.'

'You're right but who is a writer's boss? Or who should be? I don't know either, I just know that when you're trying to write something new, there are no helping hands. You're on your own.'

'We're talking about two different things. I understand the ordeals of an artist like van Gogh. One has to obliterate one's self in such a process. I'm sure there are many more artists who went on a similar journey but then faded away into nothing and we don't know about them at all. That thought terrifies me.'

'But what if they never faded away? It's just us who don't know them?'

'I think the reason you don't like your poems anymore is because you're jealous of the person who wrote them.'

I stared at her. She knew me so well and I was so comfortable with her. I'd missed such conversations in the last few years. For the first time in a long while, I was enjoying talking to someone. Your inner monologue is far more horrific than your fears. It's your weakest moments that decide the winner between you and your fears.

'I haven't read anything new from you in years. I want to see how much has changed, how much you've changed.'

'Read my stories, they're about to come out.'

'First story collection, so exciting!'

'Yes, it got postponed because of the lockdown, and I'm happy it did. They have just sent it to press, but I think it's missing a story.'

'So, are you writing it now?'

'That's the problem, I'm not sure if I'll be able to write another story or not. I'll have to talk to my editor about it.'

'Am I a part of your stories?'

'Never ask a writer that question; it's like asking a woman her age.'

Antima laughed at this, and I smiled.

'I've changed so much. Sometimes I wonder if I'm still the same person who just picked up her bag and went to Himachal with you . . . and travelled to Austria? If we looked at those pictures now, it would be hard to believe that we were the same people, walking in this deserted place now.'

A dog came running up to Antima. His tail was wagging in excitement as if he knew her. Antima got down on her knees and played with it for a while. Some more dogs gathered around her. Antima was affectionate to all of them. I've always loved to watch Antima like this from a distance. Human beings look so beautiful when completely engrossed in something. After some time, she ordered all the dogs to leave.

'Okay enough, go now.'

All the dogs obeyed her, their tails still wagging.

'Sorry,' she said.

'Oh please no, why are you apologizing? It was so sweet to watch you like that.'

She tousled my hair the same way she had with the dogs and laughed.

'Why are you laughing?'

'You need love too, just like those dogs.'

'Right? I think so too.'

'Are you dating someone?'

'Verma Madam.'

'Madam?'

'Yes, the new story I am writing. Verma Madam . . . her ghost keeps me up at night lately.'

We made it to the front of a park from the back road. There was a lone bench outside the park. I thought we should stop and sit on the bench, but before I could say something, we had passed it by. I could see silence descend over us. During this quiet period, I was thinking about Verma Madam, and Antima might be thinking about her life in Delhi. After a while, we looked at each other and realized we were very far apart. I realized that I didn't know this girl who was walking beside me. The unfamiliarity was painful. I wanted to touch her to see if she was the same Antima I had known years ago. I touched her hair and she stopped. I moved towards her, and she closed her eyes. I kissed her lightly. Yes, she is my Antima. Her lips are a source of tender affection. When I kissed her, she looked at me like she was seeing me for the first time. I took a step back. She pulled me back towards her and we kept kissing each other.

Contentment has a special scent all its own, but when we sense it, our painful pasts come hurtling back. Suddenly, that moment of happiness becomes an alien thing. Only the lingering scent remains familiar. Later, we can still smell the scent in our own breath.

We started walking back.

'Before coming here I told him I was coming to see you.'

'Oh! What did he say?'

'All you men are the same. You'll never understand how women think.'

'I'm not agreeing with him, but he wasn't wrong either.'

Antima let go of my hand.

'See . . . all of you are alike.'

'Sorry! That came out wrong.'

'No need to apologize. Women like me are used to these things. The last time I came to see you, I didn't tell him, and I felt guilty the entire time. Having a drink with an old friend felt like I was cheating on him with you. I kept wondering why I felt all this guilt. I hadn't done anything wrong. We didn't meet after that, but he kept asking about you. At first, I liked it, so I thought I should tell him that I had met you. But then I realized that he was just fishing for something. Asking things like, how much did you call me, how many times did you text me, if you're asking me to visit your house? His questions reeked of mistrust, so much so that I wanted to say that I didn't want to talk to him anymore. Does he even know me? Or does he think the moment I was out of his sight, I'd be doing all the disgusting things his head is filled up with. Last time you teased me about my boyfriend too. All of you are the same.'

When she was done talking, I apologized to her in as many ways as I could. She didn't say anything. She wasn't even crying this time. Her eyes were cold. I regretted everything I'd ever said to her. It takes a long time for small-town boys to become good human beings. No, it's not about small-town boys either. The people coming from a patriarchal background take a long time to see women as fellow humans. Although we think we've changed, patriarchy and its remnants are so deeply entrenched inside us that if we wish to change, we must maintain constant awareness in our conversations; otherwise, the venomous fangs of patriarchy will bite us when we're the most vulnerable. Like mine did just now. We're so deeply entrenched in this dirt that we've no right to look for forgiveness.

Antima sat down on the footpath. I stood beside her. I wanted to put my hand on her shoulder but didn't have the courage to do so. After some time, I sat down beside her as well.

'When you asked me to meet you today, I told him,' she said. 'I'm stuck in somebody else's house. I have nothing to do all day. I'm lonely, but to preserve my relationship, I can't even call you. He argued with me the entire day today. That's why I reached here late. I was so angry that I told him that I've met you once already. He said the same thing you had. At last, I said, *I'm going to kiss him today.*'

Her eyes were tearing up. I thought it was good she was letting go of everything. I took her hand in mine.

'Let's go home. I'll make you a nice cup of tea.'

We went home. She lay down on the sofa the moment we entered. By the time I was back with tea, she had fallen asleep. I picked her up and put her on the bed. I came out and lay down on the sofa. I was thinking about my father and how he used to behave with my mother. Then all my childhood neighbours, Raina uncle, Soni ji, Tiwari ji, Parashar babu, Chaubey ji, Dubey sahab, Lohiya ji . . . their wives were rarely seen outside the house. All of them must have learnt from their elders how to keep a woman. Generation after generation we have venerated our mothers and turned them into servants. There were two cups of tea in front of me, I didn't even want to touch them. At some point, I fell asleep thinking of my childhood.

10

A sound late at night woke me. What time was it? What day was it? Where was I? I was about to check the time but then I stopped. A bead of sweat ran down my back and I knew it must be ten past three. I sat up on the sofa. A soft breeze passed by my ear. I had a feeling that Verma Madam was somewhere near. Without wasting any time, I turned my computer on and started writing:

> Verma madam repeated her question, but Rohit kept staring at her. Verma Madam threw a piece of chalk at him which hit him in the head, only then did he come out of his trance. Everyone in the class was laughing at him. Verma Madam walked up to him.
>
> 'What's your name?'
> 'Rohit, madam.'
> 'Did it hit you?' Verma Madam asked with a smile.
> 'What?'

A boy jeered at him from the back, and the entire class started laughing. Verma Madam scolded everyone into silence. Rohit hung his head. Verma Madam touched his head and apologized to him before resuming the class. It was the first time in this village that a teacher had apologized to a student. It became a topic of discussion in the school for many days. Rohit was one of those backbenchers who always wanted to be invisible. But after the incident, everyone started paying more attention to him, especially other teachers. He loved to look out of the window during class. But he had to look at his teachers all the time now. Teachers kept asking him questions. Verma Madam felt guilty about throwing chalk at him, so she was extra nice to him, which meant she paid more attention to him, which in turn meant that Rohit was uncomfortable all the time. He found it difficult to breathe in school. One day he went to his terrace with his kite and saw that Verma Madam was having tea on the adjacent roof. By then his kite was up in the air and he couldn't just abandon it. He was already pulling it down when he heard a voice.

'Rohit, do you live here?'

'Yes madam, good evening,' he said as he pulled the kite back down.

'Oh! Why did you pull it down? Keep flying it.'

'No, it's okay,' Rohit was winding his string when he saw Verma Madam trying to jump over to his terrace. She was stuck on the boundary walls.

'Arey madam stop, I'll come over there.'

He jumped down to her side and took the cup of tea she held out to him and set it aside before giving her a hand. She jumped back to her own roof. When she jumped, he saw her chest . . . She wasn't wearing a bra. She had seen him staring. He hung his head and started for his own roof.

'Do you drink tea?' she asked.

'Yes, I do . . . but not a lot . . . just in the morning and in the evening.'

She laughed.

'So have you had the evening one yet?'

'No . . . I'll have it when I go back downstairs.'

'Wait, I'll make some for you. I want to have another cup as well.'

Without waiting for a reply, she went downstairs to make more tea. He was afraid she would ask him more questions to which he didn't know the answers. He wanted to escape this tea. He thought of running back to his house but that would be a problem when he saw her at school tomorrow. So, he stood still like a statue. Soon she was back with the tea and some biscuits. They both sat perched on the boundary wall. Rohit kept glancing at her chest, so he started staring at the sky.

'You love flying kites?'

'Yes.'

Rohit noticed a pile of thick books in the corner.

'I am pursuing a doctorate on Dinkar. Do you know who Dinkar is?'

'Yeah, he was a poet.'

'Oh! Fantastic!'

'My mother has an interest in literature, that's why I know of him.'

'Listen, let's be friends here. In school, I'm a teacher and you're a student but let's just be friends here.'

'No,' he said it so abruptly that she laughed.

'No boy has ever refused me that quickly.'

At this, Rohit laughed too. She was wearing a long white T-shirt and a green salwar. To Rohit, she looked like someone who was his own age. In school she looked older due to the saree, he thought. He felt a bit better now, lighter. He was done with his tea and was about to leave.

'You know Rohit, I feel lonely here. Whenever you're free, we should have evening tea together. I make better tea than this, I promise.'

Rohit was thinking.

'In return, I can teach you Hindi,' she added.

'No, no . . . no studying here.'

'Okay, okay, we won't talk about studying or lessons.'

'That's fine then.'

Rohit jumped back to his roof and ran inside the house. Sometime later, he came back to take his kite and string back with him. Verma Madam was watching him all this time, but he didn't look up at her.'

'I want to say something.'

I felt someone whispering in my ear. I knew that what I was writing had strayed away from what actually happened, and Verma Madam wouldn't approve of some of the things. I wanted to write further but I had to stop.

'What happened?' I whispered back.

'I was wearing a bra.'

'I know.'

'And a pair of jeans and a T-shirt.'

'Yes.'

'Dinkar? Doctorate?'

'Your actual thesis topic was boring.'

'So, you're making me interesting in the story.'

'Not at all, I just want to keep the story simple.'

'But nothing was simple.'

'It depends on how you see it.'

'What are you seeing, Rohit?'

'That I'm sitting here alone in the night blabbering to myself and writing. I can't see any further than that.'

'But there's more to the story.'

'That's for the story to decide.'

'That's what I am saying . . . let the story decide.'

'Yes, the story, not the characters.'

'But it's the characters who are living the story.'

'We're living the story.'

'You're standing at the riverbank, scared, whereas the story exists in a world underwater.'

'I won't jump.'

'I'm here to push you.'

'No.'

'You have to jump.'

'No . . .'

'Near the fort, by the riverside, under the peepal tree . . .'

'Shut up . . . shut up!'

'What are you doing?' Suddenly Verma Madam sounded different.

'What do you mean?'

'Arey, who are you talking to?'

I turned and saw that Verma Madam was not beside me
at all. I looked up to see Antima standing in the doorway,
staring at me bewildered. I told her that I was writing and
turned my computer off.

'You were arguing with someone.'

'No, nobody; why did you wake up?'

'I thought that there was someone else in the house, so I
was scared . . . then I saw you talking.'

'Sorry, sorry! My mind is a bit scattered because I've been
living here all alone. Forget it . . . I couldn't sleep so I thought
I should write something, but . . .'

I took Antima back to the bed. She was still shocked by
what she had witnessed.

'Are you okay?' she asked like a mother would to her
crazed son.

I couldn't help but laugh. Antima pulled me into bed.
I hugged her and assured her that everything was fine. She
buried her face in my chest. Soon we were both asleep.

When I woke up my eyes felt heavy. It was afternoon. I
saw that Antima wasn't beside me. She had left. The afternoon
was still like a story paused at the plot twist. I needed words.
I looked for the imagery created by those words on this
desolate afternoon. But I found nothing around my bed. I
needed to be near my writing, to bask in its warmth. I turned
my computer on and spent the whole day going between
writing and cooking. I made dal, rice and okra. I somehow
managed to burn the okra, but the rice and the dal turned
out fine. I could say the same about my writing: part of it
was burnt, but part of it had turned out well. I always feel

while writing that things would have turned out to be better if I'd written them later. That I'd have found something special. I have no idea what I'm looking for. When I read somebody else's writing, such things irk me. I prefer simple descriptions of everyday life. But in today's abnormal world, no matter how simply you write something, it doesn't turn out simple and all sorts of unusual things seem possible at any moment in time.

Nobody knows where we will go next after these weird times. Something strange is unfolding. Almost everyone is of the opinion that the lockdown should be lifted . . . if people die, let them. At least those who survive should be allowed to live their lives. I had never imagined we would come to this.

My editor mailed to tell me that he is sending the story collection to the press. I wrote back asking him to wait; there was one more story. He immediately called me.

'The stories we have are enough,' he said as soon as I picked up the call.

'No, we need one more story, the collection is incomplete without it.'

'You'll write it now?'

'I've already started, it'll be done soon.'

'Okay, I'll pause the printing for now; send it soon.'

I wish it were in my control. I swept the whole house. Mopped every corner of the floor, then went on to remove grime from various surfaces. In all this, Verma Madam's name echoed in my thoughts. Everything feels incomplete if you don't get to say certain things. Everything was clean now. I sat in front of the story for hours, dead tired from all the cleaning. Memories are like sunflowers we treasure, but we return to find them turned to dust.

Rohit's friends had started to tease him as he was always smiling for no apparent reason. He didn't know there was a constant grin on his face. His love for kites had been replaced by his anticipation for evening tea. He now prepared for these evening meetings. He knew Verma Madam loved poetry. He would go through his mother's books and look for poems which he would then note down in a diary, to make it look like an old habit. In the evening, he would open the diary and read out poems to her. He had jotted down poems by Nirala and Muktibodh, but he realized that if Verma Madam asked him anything about them, he wouldn't have an answer. So, he switched to Sarveshwar Dayal Saxena and Raghubir Sahay; he included some short poems by Bhawani Prasad Mishra as well. Whenever these poems started rhapsodising about love, his ears would go red, and he would feel a tingling sensation in his back. He recited Sarveshwar Dayal Saxena's poem 'Tum se Alag Hokar' to her. Because he really liked that poem, he knew it by heart. When he was done, Verma Madam read another one by Saxena, 'Tumhare Sath Rehkar'. He stared at her in amazement. He wasn't familiar with this poem. How could a poet write from both perspectives with such ease, like being on both banks of a river? He promised her that he'd learn this one as well.

One day his mother found him going through the books in her almirah.

'What's up with you? You've started reading a lot of books lately.'

'Yes, I'm taking tuition from Verma Madam.'

'Why didn't you tell me you needed tuition? Who will pay her fee now?'

'Arey Ma, she doesn't want any money. Verma Madam has said that I don't need to study Hindi. She's preparing me for the future. Literature which older students read . . . so it's like tuition but not really.'

'You should focus on maths instead of Hindi. You're like a lame horse in mathematics; any day now you're going to fall.'

She left the room.

From Rohit's perspective, he and Verma Madam were friends. But if Verma Madam ever placed a hand on his thigh or shoulder, a shiver ran down his body, or sometimes, if he answered a question correctly in the classroom, she would smile, and his heart would skip a beat. He had a feeling that she was now getting bored of the poems he read from his diary. He should do something else. Should he start reading hefty books? He tried to, but he always dozed off a few sentences in.

One day he was flipping through his diary when he reached a blank page, and wrote, 'I am a kite . . .' and then stared at that sentence for a long time. He returned to that sentence again and again throughout the day and stared at it. On a Sunday afternoon, when everyone in his house was asleep, he added more sentences, and after much editing, he had written his first poem ever. His joy knew no bounds. He immediately wanted to read it to Verma Madam. But before that, he went and stood in front of a mirror. It was his first poem and he wanted to practise reciting it.

I'm a kite, proud of my flight
A vast sky grins down on me
Are you the string that tethers me?
Or are you the hand that keeps me steady?
How sad it will be if the string breaks
But whose fault will it be?
Be the string,
Not the hand.
Once the string is cut
We'll fly freely in the sky
on the high of love

He thought he had written something far better than Bhawani Prasad Mishra, Sarveshwar Dayal Saxena, Raghubir Sahay and Dushyant Kumar. He took his diary and ran upstairs to the roof. He jumped from his roof and entered Verma Madam's house via the door on her roof. 'Madam,' he called out softly but got no answer. He could hear a bucket filling with water. When he followed the sound, he saw a bucket beneath a running tap in the bathroom, but Madam was not there. She was drying herself with a towel in front of the mirror. When the towel moved, he saw she wasn't wearing anything. He froze right there. He had never even seen himself without clothing. He stared at her breasts for a long time, then looked at her body. It looked like a beautiful sculpture. 'Verma Madam,' he cried out. She turned and saw him and screamed. She wrapped herself in the towel and shut the door in his face. Rohit ran back to his house and locked himself inside his room. At night when Ma came to check on him, he had a high fever and was shivering as well. For many days Rohit suffered from both fever and fear. Whenever he thought about stepping out of the house, he started shivering and his temperature rose. Verma Madam's wet, naked body refused to leave his thoughts.

'Your madam was asking about you yesterday,' said Ma when she brought him his food.

'What did she say?' he asked with such enthusiasm that his mother suspected he was pretending to be sick. But when she touched his forehead, it was still warm.

'She's going to the city for a few days and was asking about you as she hadn't seen you for many days.'

'When is she leaving?'

'She left yesterday.'

By that evening, Rohit's fever had let up. He was strolling on his roof with a bland cup of tea his mother had made. He was bored on his terrace, so he crossed over to Verma Madam's. And just like that, the tea started to taste better. He stood against the door that led to Verma Madam's house from the rooftop. He felt like it was the door to heaven. A few days ago, he had walked through this door and seen something which gave him wet dreams at night. He kissed the door and closed his eyes.

In the story, Rohit was kissing the door, and I was feeling anxious about Verma Madam. Did I have the right to write about her? Should I worry so much about a character I had created? Should I worry this much about my writing? I closed my computer and went to the kitchen for some relief. I was putting the teapot on the stove out of habit, but my mind kept seeing Verma Madam running away, covering herself with a towel.

11

Our lives are like a field of compromises where we sow the seeds of our experiences when we write. Then we sit and wait for the rain to water each seed so the saplings can grow, each one a single tale. And if we continue to water the saplings, they will eventually grow into trees of stories, which will one day provide shade to both writers and readers.

With a cup of tea in my hand, I was rehearsing the argument I'd inevitably have to have with Verma Madam one of these nights. I took a sip from the cup and wished I could tell Antima how much better I had become at making tea. When I went out to the balcony, I saw the potted plants had new flowers. Small things bring such pleasure. Blooming flowers are a beautiful surprise. I gently touched the white blossoms.

I searched for a list of songs and played them on repeat. Laura Marling, Daniela Andrade, Alexi Murdoch, Cliff Richard, Keren Ann, Simon & Garfunkel, John Prine, Leonard Cohen. The sun was setting behind some buildings.

There was a slight breeze, which made the weather outside beautiful. Today I wanted to walk to the place where the breeze carried a scent of jasmine. What must Antima be doing at this moment, I wondered. I really wanted to meet her. I wanted to read something I had written or meet her on the pretext of reading something to her but then not read anything at all. I felt like a child inside; I wanted to dance. This is the remuneration a writer gets in this country. A few moments when he can smell the jasmine before it vanishes and the moments in between, when he can dance a little. That's his life's earnings.

Pawan was making pasta in Aru's kitchen, and I was sitting on a bar stool, listening to him talk. Aru brought me some whiskey.

'Interesting, my dear friend has never made a drink for me,' Pawan joked.

'Your wine is right beside you,' said Aru, pointing to the wine. I took a sip of my drink and realized it was too strong. I added some water.

'Is it too strong?' Aru asked.

'It's fine now,' I replied.

'Come, I'll show you around the house.'

Aru's house was built on an open plan. The kitchen was part of a huge open hall, on one side of which was a tall window. A door on the other end led to the terrace with a swing. It's rare to own a house with a terrace in Mumbai. At the back of the house were two bedrooms, which I glanced at momentarily. Like a good guest, I praised everything I saw.

'You have a beautiful terrace,' I said, sitting down on the bar stool again.

'Why do you think I'm friends with her?' asked Pawan.

'If the pasta doesn't turn out well, our friendship will take a hit,' Aru retorted.

At this, Pawan shared some funny one-liners about friendship and love, and I replied with mild words of praise. Again and again, Aru spoke directly to me, but I turned the conversation in a way that Pawan felt included. In any case, Pawan was the one holding court here and it was difficult to stop him.

'Think about the situation like this, BC, or Before Covid, all of us were listening to a rock band on full volume. We couldn't understand the lyrics or figure out who the singer was. Just a constant thump . . . thump . . . thump . . . something was happening, and we had been asked to dance and enjoy it. The whole world was in a trance chanting the mantra of success and happiness. Then the pandemic came and hit the pause button. And all of us started to lose our minds. We had never experienced such silence before. Now it's nature who is dancing and we are stuck in our homes, trying to figure out a plan to bring nature to its knees.'

I laughed at Pawan's theory, but Aru said, 'That's wrong. Everyone tries to live their best lives according to their situation. We can't judge everyone like that.'

I was on my second drink. I felt light-headed after many days. For a minute, I had forgotten what sort of situation we were in. I felt distant from Pawan and Aru's argument, but I was also enjoying their conversation. Then I felt as though I saw something move in Aru's bedroom. The door to her room was half open. When I looked properly, I saw something move again. Maybe she had a very thin dog? But why hadn't I seen it when she was showing me the house? Anyway, I tried to get the thought out of my mind. Suddenly the door to her room snapped shut. I couldn't not ask.

'Do you have a pet?'

'No . . . I want one though. These days a stray cat from the building sleeps with me.'

I finished my drink and decided that I wouldn't drink any more. I realized, because I'd been isolated all these months, I'd forgotten how to be around people. I soon found myself in the washroom. I didn't want to start a third glass, but I really wanted to peek inside Aru's bedroom. I splashed water on my face, took a few deep breaths and cursed myself for behaving this way. When I came out, rather than going straight back to her and Pawan, I stopped by her bookshelf where I saw some of Márquez's novels: *One Hundred Years of Solitude, Love in the Time of Cholera,* etc. I picked one up and started to flip through it: the story of Florentino Ariza, his true love and a life spent waiting for her. Was Verma Madam the Fermina Daza of my life, the one whom I've awaited my entire life, and tried to find in everybody else? I was thinking about Antima when Aru came and stood by me. For the first time, I noticed Aru's beautiful hair. She had curly hair and some strands fell around her ears like she was wearing dangling jhumkas. Aru was tall and thin. She could wear anything and look good in it.

'I love this Márquez novel the most,' she said.

I put the book back with a smile. I rarely tell people about the books I like. I always feel that I and the books I like have a connection that is very personal. If I talk about them with other people, it'll seem as though I'm using them to attract attention. I know it's foolish, but I can't shake this feeling, so whenever something about my favourite books comes up, I prefer to change the topic.

'What do you think of it?' Aru asked.

'It's good. I know nothing about you. What do you do apart from acting?'

'There's nothing much to know. I used to work in the state bank before. I always wanted to write but everything else took precedence. Then my father passed away all of a sudden, and something changed inside me. Now, I want to do everything. Sorry, I don't like to talk about myself.'

I looked towards Pawan to see what he was doing. She thought I was looking for my drink, so she went and brought it to me. I took it from her and started looking at the bookcase to disguise my discomfort. I had nothing to say. Aru signalled at my books, which stood right next to the Márquez books.

'Don't put my books with these great books; they're not worthy at all.'

I felt a certain bitterness for my older work, which made me say such things.

'Why do you say so? These are two of my favourite books and look at what you have written.'

Aru picked up the book and showed me what I had written in it. I couldn't believe it. I looked at her to convey that I couldn't even apologize for it. She gave me a pen. I crossed out what I had written and wrote, 'I've crossed out my lies, thank you!' Before Aru could see what I'd written, I placed the book back on the shelf.

'What are you two conspiring about?' Pawan asked from the kitchen.

'Is your pasta done or not?' Aru replied.

'It definitely is!'

There was a lovely breeze. The three of us had moved to the terrace. One could see a bit of the sea from there. Pawan had cooked the pasta well. By then I had finished my third drink. Aru mimed at me if I would like another small one. I smiled in return. There's happiness in losing one's bearings. I regret things when I'm sober but after three drinks, I don't want to be conscious of anything at all. I was on my fourth drink of the night. Aru smoked a lot. I would sometimes take a few puffs of her cigarette. Pawan stuck to his own; if you asked him for a puff, he would hand it to you and give up on it. It had been a long time since I'd had a normal evening— delicious food, good friends and booze. You could sense the writer in Aru. There was something about her that was comforting. Around that you could live with your silences as well. Pawan lay on the swing. I walked over to Aru and sat down. Aru was a good hostess and asked us if we needed anything again and again.

'Did you know that Aru writes lovely poems?' Pawan asked me.

'I knew you must write well,' I said to her.

'Aru, can you read us something, please?' asked Pawan, pressing his palms together.

'Absolutely not . . . especially not in front of him.'

'Arey, you have read his poems. Shouldn't he get a chance to know how you write?' Pawan insisted.

'I understand. Sometimes it's strange to read your own writing. It's fine.' I was trying to avoid a poetry recital.

'I remember one of her poems . . . I'll recite it,' said Pawan. He sat up on the swing.

'Definitely not!' cried Aru.

'Let it go, Pawan,' I added, but Pawan was adamant. He had just started when Aru interrupted him.

'Wait, I'll read it, otherwise he'll just kill the poem.'

'Yes! Perfect!' said Pawan with a winsome smile. Aru looked at me.

'Please read,' I said with a smile. Aru took a long puff from her cigarette and began:

> To read is to pause
> To stop and watch someone walk towards you.
> Reading is not travel
> Where the place itself comes to you
> Some words give a feeling of déjà vu
> As if you had written them in the distant past
> When you read a sentence for the first time
> Its structure flows in your veins
> What's in the book had been waiting inside for ages
> And you can also see what wasn't there
> Some rooms, a jungle in disarray, a secret cellar
> All of it was a part of this house
> But we spend our whole lives trying to decorate it
> from the outside

Aru had finished her poem. I gazed at her with astonishment. I asked for a re-read. I didn't know why. But there was something in those words and the imagery they projected, that by the end I was just looking at her while she read, as if in a trance. I felt that those words described how I had been feeling for a long time. I could have written that poem. Aru had just started again when I heard something move. A deer jumped out of the inner room and came to stand among us.

I looked up at Aru. She was immersed in her poem. Pawan was lighting another cigarette. I listened to the poem while looking at the deer who was slowly approaching me. When the deer was close, I placed a hand on its head. It was like touching something of my own, something personal. I closed my eyes. I knew this deer and it knew me.

When I opened my eyes, everything was calm. My hand was up in the air. Aru was sitting next to me and staring at me. Pawan was staring at me too, from the swing. I brought my hand back down.

'It's a beautiful poem. You write so well.'

I said this as if I was completely immersed in her poem and my lifted hand was proof of that. I finished my drink and said my goodbyes. Pawan was quite drunk. He couldn't stand up from the swing, but he tried to stop me all the same. Aru didn't say much. She came with me to the door. I pressed the button for the lift, and we waited for it. Waiting is strange.

'Did you really like the poem?' asked Aru, breaking the silence.

'Yes, it was beautiful.'

'Now you've seen where I live. I'm a great hostess. You must come for a cup of coffee whenever you want.'

'Of course.'

I entered the lift and pressed the button. As it started to descend from the sixth floor, I could see Aru standing in the light, while I was getting buried in darkness. I opened the doors as soon as the elevator reached zero and stumbled towards my house.

12

I lay in bed with my eyes shut. My body started to shut down systematically. Everything I had experienced during the day came back to me like an echo in the mountains. The lizards, the green thread, my father's breath, the deer, a mole on a neck. Then suddenly I felt a patch of quiet growing somewhere on my body, maybe from the spot where goosebumps start to rise, then spreading all around. Falling asleep felt like the most pleasurable thing that had happened that day.

Maybe Antima was nobody; just a mole I had seen peeking out from behind a muffler on a December day in Delhi. Maybe Pawan was a splinter that had pierced my finger when I was a child, which I was now attempting to remove. Maybe Aru was a girl reading Márquez's *Love in the Time of Cholera*, someone I had encountered during my travels. When I tried to speak with her, I could only ask her for a lighter to light my cigarette. Maybe my father passed away long ago and it's the guilt over my relationship with him

which is eclipsing the whole story. Maybe I am still Rohit,
still lying somewhere wrapped in Verma Madam's towel,
whereas she was a character in a novel I once read. That's
when I saw the frightened eyes of the deer and in those eyes,
I saw horrors both foreign and familiar. I had not cleaned
the house in days. There were clothes in the bathroom to be
washed but I was again putting that task off for tomorrow.
It was hunger that made me do everything in the kitchen
on time. At times, I got busy watching a bird; sometimes a
thirsty crow would come to my balcony looking for water
and I would be distracted watching him hop around. The
world had shrunk so much that every small thing seemed
big and everything huge happening around the world
didn't affect us anymore. We heard one weird news story
after another. Everyone was waiting for the next unexpected
thing to happen. Just for our entertainment, we wanted
more to happen, so that we could find in it a reason for
our existence. Everyone wanted to be a participant. No one
wanted to sit on the sidelines as a mere witness. In that bid
to participate, people propagated every rumour that was not
directly related to their own tragedy, although everything
was connected to us. If we step back a bit and pay attention,
we'll see that there's a huge difference between what we
say and what we do. The more I wanted to stay away from
certain things, the more I found myself smack in the middle
of them. This happened more when I called Salim. He liked
to read up on each and every issue and then discuss it with
me. I listened to whatever he had to say without much
input. All my inputs came from a majoritarian perspective.
The good thing is that we are both atheistic, so we land at
the same place in the end.

For a while, I kept thinking that something was amiss when I suddenly realized that there was no music. So, I put my earlier playlist on repeat, and everything was perfect again. I wanted to go back to Verma Madam's story, but her participation was necessary for me to write further, and she was nowhere to be found. In the story, she had gone to the city but was refusing to come back. I woke up every night and checked the wall clock in the drawing room only to realize that it was later than ten past three. I had created a superstition that if I didn't get up at ten past three, the story wouldn't proceed. That time was like consent, for which I kept asking Verma Madam so I could take the story further. But she was stubborn and wouldn't budge and I had no other choice but to be faithful to my character.

My father called. He said that the whole world is cursed by the heavens. I couldn't understand what he meant. So, I asked him, 'How are you bringing the heavens into this?' His reply was that Kashmir is heaven and we have hurt it a lot, so we are bound to be cursed by it. Salim told me that if there was anything in the newspaper about Kashmir, my father would read the story multiple times and then stare at the associated photograph the whole day as if looking for himself in the picture. Nobody knows exactly what happened to him in Kashmir. The last time he went there was to sell his house for nothing. He then noted down the phone numbers of some of his friends in a small yellow diary he kept under his pillow. He would sometimes take it out, call up his friends and argue with them in Kashmiri. Or maybe they were just talking but there would be so much excitement in his voice that it felt like he was fighting with someone. When he argued with his friends, his face reddened to a shade much like the apples of his beloved Kashmir. I really wished to learn Kashmiri, but my father was against it. He was of the opinion that if I wanted to learn a language, I should learn English. He never talked to me in Kashmiri, and I developed a hatred for English as a result. Some afternoons, letters would arrive from the Valley, all written in Urdu. I found the writing and the script so beautiful, I kept looking at them. My father would let me play with the letter before hiding it away in his secret closet. He was my father and his secret world lived inside our house. Whenever he opened his almirah, we would get a glimpse of that hidden world. Even when I asked him a lot of questions, he would only talk about the snow and the sky. Otherwise, he would retire to the restroom and that would be the end of the discussion. Whenever I brought up Kashmir in my arguments while my mother was alive, she would silence me. My mother had blank spaces regarding Kashmir in her memory, which she preferred to keep that way. After Ma, my father fell ill, and Kashmir vanished from our conversations. These days he has started to bring it up again.

After Ma passed away, I brought my father to Mumbai. Soon we reached the conclusion that it wasn't possible to live together, especially in these small Mumbai flats. He returned to the village. Salim was a rickshaw puller. Soon he became his regular rickshaw guy. They became friends, and before we knew it, Salim became an important part of his life. Salim took over all the responsibilities of my father from me. Maybe he was my stillborn brother, come to life. At first, this became a reason for guilt surrounding my relationship with my father, but now I think this has given rise to more affection between us. He would ask Salim about my well-being and I would do the same.

13

Aru messaged me. *It's drizzling outside; can you see?* I went and stood on the balcony but there was no rain. There was a chill in the air. I didn't reply to her. I just stood there and stared at my deserted surroundings. At times your life looks so disorganised in hindsight. Suddenly, you see a day from the past hanging in the air in front of you and you pity it. In such moments, I wish I too had a cupboard like my father where I could keep all my past in an organized manner. At least then I wouldn't have to confront these days hanging here and there with no rhyme or reason.

Soon I found myself walking on the deserted road at night. I didn't feel like doing anything, but my body wanted to tire itself out. Worrying about not forgetting to carry a mask had made me forget to bring my phone instead. Mumbai had never been this deserted. Walking on these roads gave me a feeling that I was walking inside my body. It was so quiet that I could hear my own footsteps like somebody was following me. In the light from the lamp posts, my shadow kept changing positions. One moment it would be ahead of me and the next it would start trailing behind. At times, I wasn't one person but two but then it so happened that my own shadow seemed to be eating my shoe. I could see some dogs running around. Some people stepped out of dark corners, only to disappear into other similarly dark corners. A police car . . . an ambulance . . . Like us, the nights in this city had changed as well. As usual, I was looking for the more deserted and dark corners. In this city full of people, we always search for empty spaces. During all these days passing by haphazardly, I was constantly on the lookout for places to write. I wished I were in the mountains. A good place to write is like a river, flowing along, where one can lie in the current without ever drowning. At that moment, I was less walking and more floating. I should have texted Aru back. Whenever somebody threatens to come even a bit closer, I feel the waters tremble, both in the river and inside me. The tranquillity inside me was breaking. What hypocrisy, when someone is beginning to enter my world, I look like I am welcoming them inside my world. But soon that person finds themselves in a deserted ruin with dilapidated buildings, right out of a war-torn city. And I slink away, leaving them to wander alone. I've done this so many times that I don't feel regret anymore, just disgust at my behaviour. These days I get nervous whenever I meet someone new and want to stop them right at the door. Like I've stopped Aru at the door, and I know that I should have replied to her. I was frustrated with myself. 'Shut up,' I shouted at myself. Had I gone mad? Shouting out loud alone on the road. And who did I want to shut up?

At a far-off crossroads, some people were looking at me and for no reason, I waved at them and then took another road to slip away like a thief. It's good that I was wearing a mask, nobody would recognise me behaving like this. Who knows me here anyway? How many people even care to know writers in this country?

What's the time? What day is it? Antima is flying back to Delhi tomorrow. I wanted to meet her before she departed. I didn't have my phone on me right then, but I wished I did because I wanted to call everyone up and listen to all their stories. How did their day go? I wished to know everything in great detail. Why was I not like Salim? Why could I not be the son my father always wanted? My mother always scolded me to improve me. Why did I not become completely perfect? I am a writer, but I don't look like a writer. What do writers even look like? I didn't really want to be seen but I also wanted people to see me. I ran a hand across my head and took a deep breath. Aru was still standing at the door waiting to be let in and I was hindering her. Or maybe she didn't want to come in but because I was in her way, she was more curious to peek inside. I liked Pawan. I couldn't betray him. I liked it when Pawan talked but I also wished to run away the moment he stopped talking. Maybe Pawan could remove this splinter from my finger. I was stuck in a net of contradictions. The threads scraped my body and I dug into the wounds looking for a truthful story.

I had walked far away from home. I decided to take a shortcut back. The wind was soothing. I took a deep breath again. I needed to get it together. I was straying from the story. I started thinking about the story and my brisk walk soon slowed down to a stroll and then I stopped walking altogether. I found myself standing in front of an ancient, dilapidated house. One could see a dim light shining from its two back rooms. This place was weirdly familiar to me. I pushed the broken gate and it creaked open. Soon I was inside the house. The main door of the house was broken, and somebody had nailed two planks across it. I tried to peek inside but couldn't see anything on the other side of the door. I knew this house. I walked towards the other end. As I walked, the crunching of dry leaves echoed in my ears. It seemed like I had entered a jungle of the past. The light from the lamp post fell on a shattered window. When I tried to peek inside from another window, I saw a dust-covered bukhari burn in the middle of the house. The kangri had fallen on the floor and Ma was trying to collect the pieces of coal that had fallen from it. Her hands were burning, and yet she was trying to put the embers back. The walls of the house, partially visible in the smoke and light, were calligraphed with Urdu, with words from some letter which had arrived for my father from Kashmir. In a corner, my father was trying to read the writing on the wall. Music erupted from the Kashmiri words. Mumbling away in Kashmiri, he suddenly spotted me standing in the window. I stumbled and fell. Fearfully I tried to gather myself up and leave but there was a noise at the back of the house. Across the verandah, in the corner occupied by the banyan tree, I heard someone and started walking towards them. All of a sudden I saw two shiny eyes staring at me. I took a few steps in that direction and stopped. The eyes moved towards me and then that same deer jumped in front of me. I screamed and started to run home, jumping over a wall that stood in the way. I slowed down near my house but was still moving fast.

I needed a long peaceful sleep. I wanted my bed. I needed the broad shoulders of my father. I wanted my mother's lap.

I was breaking down and turning into a child. I wanted to shout and tell everyone I was just a kid and that I hadn't grown up yet . . . I wanted to weep. I started to run again. I don't remember when I reached home and fell on my bed and went to sleep. I don't remember any of it. There's a lot of confusion there but it's all sidelined by sleep.

> The house collapses in front of my eyes.
> The nearer we move to save it,
> The farther it seems.
> We can only see disembodied faces,
> appearing and vanishing in the settling dust.
> Where do the lines on the faces start,
> And where do the cracks in the house end,
> The difference is blurred.
> While collecting his mother's bones in the ashes,
> He had found some remnants of his house too.

I don't remember at what point before falling asleep I turned on my computer and wrote this poem. I hate poems. I didn't want to write another poem, so why did I write this? Was it because of the poem Aru read to me? Did I want to write a poem to invite her in? Did I want to take advantage of her with a poem? I hate poems so much. I deleted those lines and swore that I wouldn't write another line of poetry. I need to focus on the story.

14

I texted Antima that I wanted to meet her. She replied a while later that she would come to meet me and that her flight was leaving late at night. She didn't say when, and I didn't ask. I could sense from her replies that she was busy. I cleaned the whole house. Sweeping, mopping, dishes, laundry, I did everything with my head down, automatically. Is it possible to not think about anything, though? But I didn't want to see whatever I was thinking. Every thought that came to my mind was like a water bubble; it would emerge, plead its case and burst into nothingness. Just to be replaced immediately by another. I was vigorously cleaning my house as if trying to push all these bubbles from each and every corner of my mind. My phone rang, but I could still see some thoughts stuck in the corners of my house, so I didn't pick up the call. I was cleaning like a lunatic. When finally the house was clean and empty, I lay down on the floor. I'm always amazed at how the smallest things in the world are connected to the largest things. Even a leaf represents the entire universe in its structure. Whereas every leaf differs from another in its structure. There's so much diversity and yet somehow, everything is alike.

I reached out and picked up my phone, and there was a missed call from Pawan. I called him back.

'Hello . . . How are you?' His tone was healthy and crisp.

'I'm good.'

'Are you coming for the evening walk today?'

'I have to meet someone in the evening; I'll come if that gets cancelled.'

'I need to talk to you. If not in the evening, then we'll meet tomorrow.'

'Is it urgent?'

'I'll tell you when we meet.'

As soon as I was done talking to Pawan, I saw Aru standing at my doorstep. How long could I hold her off at the doorway? Was I only attracted to Aru because Pawan liked her? And I knew myself, if I didn't meet Pawan now, I'd find myself in front of Aru. I texted him and asked if we could meet now. His reply came instantly: *In an hour?* I asked: *Under my house?* He replied with an *okay*.

No matter how much we try, can we ever be sure we have cleared out all our mistakes? After every mistake, we swear not to do it again. We'll make space for new mistakes, but our old ones keep crawling back to their old familiar spaces. Anything new is difficult, even if it's an error. Whenever I step out to make new mistakes, I return with the old ones weighing me down. Even new errors avoid old life, running on the same track.

Pawan stood in front of me. I had waited for him for a long time. He asked for water the moment he arrived. I went back upstairs and brought him down a bottle of water. He drank like he had been thirsty for ages. When I saw him drinking water, I realized I was thirsty too. He was holding onto the water bottle, and before I could ask him for it, he asked, 'Isn't it very hot today?'

'Yes, it's way hotter this year,' I replied, waiting for the right moment to ask for the bottle of water.

'You live in a good area,' he said.

'Didn't you come to talk about something important?'

'Yes . . . last night I killed the last baby lizard from that family.'

I had no idea what to say to this. I motioned for him to give the water bottle back. At that moment, I just wanted to drink water. As he returned the bottle, I saw tears in his eyes. I ignored my thirst and asked him, 'What's wrong?'

'My name is not Pawan.'

I felt like he was one of the characters from my story who had come to take up a fight with the author as he didn't like the name he was given.

'If not Pawan, then what is it?'

'Dushyant . . .'

I had heard that name somewhere. There was a face attached to that name. And I knew that face. But that face couldn't be the same as Pawan's. Does the way one's face looks change on the basis of one's name?

'Dushyant? You don't look like Dushyant to me.'

Pawan took the water bottle back from me and chugged the rest. I was still thirsty.

'What does Dushyant look like?'

'Dushyant looks like Dushyant, you're Pawan.'

It felt weird to tell Pawan that he was Pawan. I became silent. Pawan needed to find a way to explain himself. When he finally found his bearings he said, 'When I came to Mumbai some twenty years ago, I used to live in Dahisar. The colony in Dahisar East was near the rail tracks. One night, my friend and I were walking on the tracks on our way home. I was narrating the story of the film *Sholay* to him, complete with dialogues. We were so lost in the story and so tired from the day's work that we never saw the train coming towards us. When I saw the train, its movement hypnotised me. My friend got off the track instantly, but I stood there staring at the approaching train. I felt I had never experienced such a beautiful moment before. It was magical, death coming at you at such speed and your acceptance of it. I closed my eyes in anticipation of the collision but just before the train could touch me, my friend pushed me aside. As I fell away, there were drops of blood on my face . . . My friend had been hit by the train. It took me a while to gather my senses and then I saw parts of his body scattered about.'

Pawan sounded like he was choking up, but he had just stopped to catch his breath.

'I took his remains back to his village, Satna. I stayed with his family for thirteen days, but I couldn't gather the courage to tell them anything. I couldn't bear his family's pain. I realized I must do something for them. I went back to my village and officially changed my name to Pawan. It had been his name. I went back to his village, but I wasn't Pawan for his family. When I returned to Mumbai, I tried my best to become Pawan. I started hanging out with his theatre friends. I tried to do the things he would have. I had come here to become an actor, but Pawan was more interested in plays. Because of him, I did theatre. The same kind of theatre he would have wanted to do. But after all these years, I'm tired of pretending to be Pawan. Dushyant wanted a simple life– marriage, lots of kids, household problems, a refrigerator, a television, a washing machine, a few jokes, friendships. His favourite song was, *"Chota sa ghar hoga, baadlo ki chaanv mein . . . Asha diwani usmein baansuri bajayegi, hum hi hum chamakenge taaro ki us chaanv mein . . ."* After some time I couldn't decide who I had wronged more, Pawan or Dushyant. I want to go back and start again from the point when I left Dushyant on those tracks.'

Pawan was not looking at me anymore. He was looking for a way to escape unharmed from the web he had spun.

'Last night when I tried to kill that baby lizard, it didn't die. It fell on the ground and lay there thrashing with pain. I hit it repeatedly with my slipper but somehow life still stuck to some part of its body, and it wasn't letting go. I kept hitting it, but some parts of the body still moved. After the train collision, Pawan's body was cut in half. As I reached him, I saw that he was looking at me. He was also looking at his body, which had been cut at the waist. When I collected his body parts and put them on a cart, he was still looking at the detached legs that I had laid beside him. Finally, I took off my shirt and covered his face.'

I stared upwards and saw a bird sitting in a tree. I was hoping that the bird would chirp and break the silence. She danced around on the tree, as if mocking me, but didn't make a peep. The atmosphere was still; there was no wind. I was still thirsty and because of Pawan's story, my stomach was churning. When the bird flew away silently, I told Pawan that I was going to get some cigarettes. He nodded. As soon as I reached home, I drank an entire bottle of water.

While telling me the story, had he been Pawan or Dushyant? How much of Pawan was inside Dushyant? How much of Dushyant's weight was Pawan carrying around? I always thought of Pawan as a jolly person, always waiting for an opportunity to laugh, but that sort of waiting can be like a tree with deep roots. I handed over a cigarette to Pawan. He took a puff and said, 'Do you know how bad the situation in Brazil is? Right now, India is at the seventh number. How to tell our citizens that this is not something you win at?'

And he started laughing at his own joke as if everything that he'd said before this had been said by somebody else. I was having difficulty even pretending to laugh. Then Pawan moved on to his theory, that this virus must have been discovered by a nature lover. It had finally made human beings sit at home and had infected 70 per cent of humans. No animal had been affected by this. I was waiting for him to be done with his cigarette. I wished he would talk more about Pawan and Dushyant, but he had moved long past them. As he was leaving, Pawan tried to hug me. I hesitated at first but then gave in. He held me for a while, and I held them both.

15

The sky was a deep pink today. It looked like it would rain. A beautiful breeze was blowing. In the boredom of the heat, even the trees were unable to contain their excitement for the rain. I came out and stared at the sky. What time was it? What day was it? How weird was it that we couldn't keep hold of anything? Everything seemed to be passing by without us living it. Why couldn't we set a few days aside for ourselves, and if not days, seconds? A few moments from the past to be relived, as and when desired. My body wanted to swallow this sky whole and cover the darkness inside me with this deep pink.

I cleaned my house, changed the bedsheets and pillowcases, cooked food for two people and set everything up on the table. I checked my phone, but there was nothing from Antima. When I called her, I got a busy tone. I texted her too but didn't get a reply. I poured myself a drink and sat down to work on my story. I could feel Verma Madam's absence from it. She was nowhere. I would go to type something, but my hands would shake. One has to be cruel to be able to write. Should I write about the riverbank and the peepal tree? Should I jump into the river whose depths have scared me into strolling along its banks? I got up and started walking around the room as if that would help answer my questions. I stood in front of the mirror and asked myself, can I write about this? and waited for some sort of permission, but none came. I finished my drink and sat down in front of my computer again. When all the questions are gone, you have to deal with the answers. I typed a word: 'Dushyant . . .' Writing it down made me anxious. I got up and made myself another drink. I didn't go back to the story. Why did I type Dushyant? Could I write about that? I stood at a distance, staring at what I had written but I didn't have the courage to go near it. I took a long gulp of my drink and went back to writing. I was just about to type when someone spoke . . .

'His name was not Dushyant.'

I was happy beyond measure, but I didn't move my hands away from the keyboard. She had arrived.

'I know.'

'Comfort and discomfort are the same thing. Everything around you is just one thing. The past is nothing . . . everything is a part of the present. Whatever you are hiding inside you, it's happening now, right now you can shirk it off by calling it history. It's the past that beats like a heart within the present.'

'His name is Dushyant.'

'His name . . .' Verma Madam was about to say, but I interrupted her.

'Don't.'

'Okay, Dushyant it is.'

I was very cautious with my answers. I didn't want her to leave. This story needed her. It was impossible for me to go down this road on my own.

'The foundation of my writing isn't strong enough.'

'And you want me to comfort you?'

'I believe I have the right to expect that much from you.' I was begging her. She touched my hair.

'You're on the right path,' she said. I resumed writing.

When Verma Madam came back from the city, Dushyant came with her. Rohit didn't know about Dushyant. Whenever he saw her in the classroom his heart raced. She taught the class so casually you wouldn't know she had been away for a while. When Rohit looked at her, he imagined she was wearing a towel instead of a saree and that it was about to fall off. Whenever she turned towards the blackboard to write something, he could feel something happening between his thighs. Rohit was breathing heavily, his hand was curled into a fist and was trying to stop whatever was happening between his thighs by clenching his jaw. His bench-mate looked at him. Rohit signalled to him that he had a stomach ache. The boy raised his hand. Before Rohit could stop him, the raised hand had caught Verma Madam's attention.

'What is it, Bunty?'

'Madam, Rohit's stomach is hurting.'

Probably for the first time in a long time, she looked straight at Rohit. He wanted to be swallowed by the earth and then disappear. She asked the boy to sit down and resumed teaching.

Upon reaching home, Rohit went directly to the bathroom. He looked at himself while bathing. Something was changing in his body. He could feel some heat between his legs. When he touched his penis, he could feel it growing. He turned the tap on and sat under it. He felt lighter when he came out.

On the pretext of flying a kite, he took his torn-up kite to the terrace. Dushyant and Verma Madam were having tea on the adjacent balcony.

'Oh, so this is Rohit,' Dushyant said as soon as he arrived.

Rohit saw Dushyant for the first time: he was tall and lean with unruly hair, and a wispy beard. Rohit smiled at him. Verma Madam motioned for him to come over. He was surprised. He threw his kite away and jumped over to their terrace.

'Namaste sir, namaste madam,' he said.

'Rohit, this is Dushyant, a very good friend of mine. He's a brilliant poet. And this is a promising student from my class, Rohit. My neighbour and only friend in this village.'

'Hello, Rohit.'

Rohit shook Dushyant's hand. Dushyant's hand was softer than his. Rohit held onto it longer than needed.

'Rohit loves poetry. Dushyant was just reading a very beautiful poem to me that he wrote. Please read it again . . . Rohit would like it as well.'

Verma Madam poured a cup of tea for Rohit. She and Dushyant looked at each other and smiled. He started reading the poem:

You induce a myriad of colours in my life
You contain so many colours
Before the, you turn blue
And I go red, before you
You know the deceit of your colours
I steal the ones which conceal
You and I
When you leave me
I turn blue
And when I see you with someone else
I turn colour blind
And when you hug me
I turn to water
What colour is water
Whenever I say your name
I see colours
These days when we miss each other
It doesn't result in hiccups
It rains instead . . .

Dushyant held Verma Madam's hand as he read the poem. Rohit could imagine Dushyant's soft hands caressing her naked body. When Dushyant was done reading, Verma Madam clapped. Rohit had barely heard the thing. He clapped with her. She was trying to persuade Dushyant to read some more of his poems. Rohit did the same. After some insistence, he gave in. But Rohit couldn't understand them. All his attention was focused on their hands. After each poem, Dushyant would kiss Verma Madam and Rohit would take a deep breath. There was a light breeze, and she was wearing a saree. Rohit's attention wandered to her belly or to her chest. He could feel something happen between his thighs again. Suddenly he realized she had noticed him looking. Dushyant was reading his poem, when Rohit interrupted him, 'I have written a poem too.'

Dushyant stopped reading. Verma Madam looked uncomfortable.

'Sure, let Dushyant finish his poem first, then you can read yours.'

'No, I want to read it now,' Rohit said. They were both uncomfortable now.

'Let Dushyant finish his poem, Rohit.'

'I've already read many poems today. Let's listen to him as well,' Dushyant said.

Rohit could sense she was unhappy.

'Should I start?' he asked her.

'Yes!' she said tersely.

Rohit started reading in a shaky voice:

I'm a kite, proud of my flight
A vast sky grins down on me
Are you the string that tethers me?
Or are you the hand that keeps me steady?
How sad it will be if the string breaks
But whose fault will it be?

Rohit's throat was drying up. He stopped reading.
'That's it . . . it was a good poem . . . well done!' Dushyant said and clapped.
'There's more,' Rohit said, looking up at Verma Madam.
'Then why did you stop? Finish it,' she said.
Rohit hung his head and read on:

Be the string,
Not the hand.
Once the string is cut
We'll fly freely in the sky
And together we'll dance on high

Rohit was silent again. He nodded towards Dushyant to signal that he was done. Dushyant repeated the last line and praised his work. When Verma Madam applauded his poem, he held her hand, squeezed it lightly and then kissed it, the same way Dushyant had. Dushyant couldn't stop himself from laughing at this. Verma Madam pulled her hand back but even she couldn't control her laughter. Rohit didn't want to behave like this. He couldn't understand why he had acted out something that was supposed to be inside his head. He had no control over himself. He was looking at both of them laughing and it irritated him.

My phone rang. I was stuck at Rohit's irritation. It stopped ringing. I was about to resume writing when it rang again. I could still feel Verma Madam's presence around me. I was surprised she hadn't said anything so far. The phone wouldn't stop ringing so I picked it up to put it on silent mode, I saw it was Antima. I remembered she was coming to visit me.

'Where are you? I cooked for you, when are you coming?'

'I'm at the airport, Rohit, and my flight has already left.'

'What do you mean? When was your flight? You didn't tell me anything.'

Antima was quiet. With all my questions, I hadn't heard her sobbing.

'What happened?' I asked.

I didn't say anything more. Whenever she tried to say something, it came out as sobs and then everything went quiet. What day was it? What time was it? My room was dark. I'd forgotten to turn on the light. When I looked towards my computer, I saw Verma Madam was sitting in front of it. She was typing something. I wanted to stop her but I couldn't leave Antima sobbing alone. In the darkness, I could only see her outline illuminated by the screen. Her cheeks shone as if wet. Between Antima's sobs and a tearful Verma Madam, I could only hear the sound of typing.

'I couldn't go back to him. I couldn't muster enough courage to board the flight to Delhi,' said Antima after composing herself a bit.

'Listen, come to my house immediately.'

'No Rohit, I don't want to come to you.'

'So, what will you do?'

'I've booked an Uber and I'll go back to my friend's place. Rohit, I am tired, I've spent the whole day arguing. I want to sleep now.'

'Okay, I understand.'

'No, you don't. I'll see you soon once everything is fixed. Sorry Rohit, good night.'

'Take care, good night.'

I can't stand to see Antima crying like this. There are some people who you could never imagine crying. That's the issue with phone calls. The image in your mind of the person you're talking to is completely different and doesn't match with the voice coming from the other side. So, you're only consoling the face you can visualise. Anything you say rings hollow.

I couldn't tolerate the dark. When I turned on the light, I saw that my computer was shut, and the room was looking back at me with months of emptiness inside it. I couldn't stare at the void for long and turned the lights out.

Why do I keep trying to sift through the ashes of my life? Why do I have so much love for Antima? Whereas Aru is a living story I'm resisting. I'm tired of the pity I feel at the end of relationships. The past relationships haven't left yet, and the new ones are already waiting at the door. I wish I could show them my wretchedness before they came in. I don't want to start anything new but the emptiness inside me always puts me in front of a new beginning. I start seeing words and pictures there and all the doors are opened. I have no control over Aru's entry in my life anymore. It's too late now. *Coffee?* I texted Aru and kept staring at my phone for a long time.

16

Last night I had a dream about Kashmir. I called my father in the morning but didn't get to tell him about it. He sounded tired. And soon he handed the phone over to Salim.

'Things are in a bad way here. In the last few days, a lot of people have died in the village but there are no reports about it anywhere. They're being more stringent.'

'Yes, it's like that everywhere.'

'The virus of hatred is much more terrifying brother. The other day I was coming back here, I was wearing a face mask. I had done some shopping and was carrying the items back. Some policemen stopped me, asked my name and then slapped me. I was so angry but I know why they did what they did. I rarely go out now.'

'Why didn't you tell me?'

'What would I say? If I told you everything, I'd have to call twice a day. What can you do . . . they're in a position to slap me and so they do it.'

Everything feels pointless around Salim.

'Do you know the name of the policeman?'

'Let it go, bhai. Oh, I heard a black man was killed in America. There are a lot of protests going on.'

'And here I was thinking their country is more evolved than ours. Are they still stuck on black and white?'

'Yes,'

'What's the point then, if forward nations are like that, won't we just stay like this, even when we're developed?'

'That's not true, there are many countries like New Zealand, Canada, etc., where the conditions are better. If there are bad people, there are good ones too. It's just that vile things are shared more on social media, than good things.'

'But isn't it wrong . . .?'

'Good people and good things are never performative or dramatic. And in today's idle life, everyone needs some drama. And everyone has to suffer the consequences.'

'Oh, the other day, I made great chicken. Your father really loved it, but after that, he was making multiple trips to the toilet.'

'You must have made it spicy.'

'But that's how he likes it. These days he doesn't get out of bed at all. Just sleeps day and night. You should tell him to at least walk around the house if nothing else. If what you eat isn't digested, how can you eat more?'

Salim could change topics very quickly. You might be talking to him about anything and his brain would wander off to something else entirely. One is always playing catch-up while talking to him. He says everything on his mind out loud, and the minute he does that, he seems to be free of the problem. And maybe he does feel free . . . at least I chose to believe he did.

Sometimes while writing, it seems like we're writing the same dialogue again and again, or our stories are roaming around the same territory over and over. So, we take a break from it, travel, read new writing, watch good films and devote time to our relationships. Touch, vision, taste, smell . . . Whatever goes in will come out. Our outer persona is nourished by what we take in. In this information-heavy age, we end up taking in so much hatred and treachery, that we become shrivelled and dry. What can we do? Why can't we do anything? Sometimes I feel like dropping everything and starting a journey to fix the world. But I keep coming back to the same question. What am I? What's my contribution to this world? The answers keep changing and a sense of helplessness sets in. The internal struggle never ends: what is our contribution, how does it matter and how much? These questions cut into our contribution, which in the end dies at the hands of problems.

17

The sun was about to set. A small bird appeared in front of me like a joyful moment lost to time. But as soon as I immersed myself in its beauty, it flew away. I never know how sad I am supposed to be when joy fades away. If I'd captured that moment on camera, would it have brought me the same amount of happiness every time I looked at the photo of the bird? It was a beautiful sunset. I pulled out my phone and clicked a picture. When I looked at the photo, it resembled the sunset in front of me, but something was amiss. This sunset lacked an end to its story, its beauty was marred by the pandemic, and it was racked with our internal turmoil. No photograph can capture what's unfolding at that time. I deleted the picture from my phone. I turned back only to realize that Aru had clicked my photo.

'The sky is beautiful today,' she said. She was embarrassed. I was sitting on a swing on her rooftop. She poured coffee for us both from the pot. Its aroma surrounded us. I could see the evening merging into the night on Aru's face, her light was entering my darkness. After a long while I felt truly weightless, like being rejuvenated after a long and deep slumber. Coffee brought a smile to my lips.

'You seem to be in a good mood today,' Aru said.

'It's a beautiful evening, there's a pleasant chill in the air after many days.'

'It's about to rain.'

'The forewarning of somebody's imminent arrival is always beautiful.'

'I have a wish. I am only saying it today because you're in a good mood.'

'Yes, tell me.'

'First promise me you'll do what I ask you to do.'

'Okay, sure.'

She went and brought my book of poems. She placed it in my lap.

'There's a poem on page forty-two. I've always wanted you to read it to me. Please.'

I must have been really happy that day. I didn't feel as bad as usual while turning the pages of my book. I found the poem.

'Should I start?'

'Wait, I want to light a cigarette first.'

She was ready with her cigarette and her coffee. I saw her take a few puffs before I started:

I am a thief
I see myself being used up
But still, I save a little bit of myself
with middle-class tricks
We are free, we can do anything

We are mere labourers in this bazaar of freedom
From my make-believe
I steal a breath of relief
I am a thief
I take a jug of water
To my dried-up river every day
With that, I produce waves in the dry bed
I tempt the dry dirt of the riverbed
With dreams of water
I am a thief
And I teach everyone around me
The art of stealing

Aru opened her eyes when I finished reading the poem.

'I wrote it ages ago, I don't know any more why I wrote it,' I said.

'I wanted you to read it to me because when I first read it, I thought; I could've written this as well. You denigrate your own thoughts but then you see the same things in a book and kick yourself about not writing it yourself when you had the chance.'

'I feel the same about travelling. I see a city and think I already know it. Why didn't I come here before, I wonder? It was waiting for me here all this time.'

'For me, it's books and people. You're the first person I've read and met, and then wondered why I hadn't earlier?'

If it were any other day, I would be embarrassed by this praise. But today felt like a new day, a day of many firsts, so I kept talking to her. Suddenly Aru saw something on her phone and stood up with a start.

'Sorry, you must excuse me. I had a Zoom call with my family, and I forgot about it. I can't ignore it.'

And she ran inside her house. I walked along her terrace and finished my coffee. Aru texted me from her room, *ten minutes only*. I told her to take her time. I received an email from my editor. It said, *how far along are you in the story? Can you do it faster? This is the best time to publish a book.* I put the phone back in my pocket. I had written something the day before, but how far along was I in the story? Surprisingly I didn't remember much from last night. Antima was supposed to visit but she didn't. She had gone back to Delhi instead. No, no, she couldn't go back. Did she really not go, or had I just stopped her from going in my story? For the first time, I couldn't decide where my life ended, and the writing began. Should I call Antima and ask her if she was in Delhi or Mumbai? No, I should first read what I had written yesterday; maybe nothing had happened last night. I wiped my hand across my face as if to remove yesterday's residue. I took a deep breath. When I looked down at the road below, I saw somebody standing near the lamppost. When I looked more closely, I saw a deer standing there. I walked to the other side of the terrace. I remembered I had seen Verma Madam typing on my computer. Why hadn't I turned my computer on this morning? Why hadn't I checked what she had written? Was I really losing my mind? How crazy can a writer get? I was dreaming that a character I had created was writing my story.

Aru came back with two glasses of wine.

'This is the only way to apologize. I've been saving this bottle for ages, to open on a special occasion.' She sat at one end of the swing.

'I'll not refuse, but I won't be able to have more than a glass. I've reached the age where I should keep my drinking in check.'

Aru laughed and nodded in agreement. The wine was really good. She asked about my taste in music. 'Anything slow would work,' I said. With the help of the wine and the music, our conversation moved between the weather and these difficult days. Talking to her reminded me of all the novels I'd read. When she spoke, I could sense lethargy and something like humiliation and amidst all that she kept on smoking. Her hand covered her face when she laughed. If I said something flattering to her, she turned her head away and wouldn't look back till I stopped. I felt if I touched her, she would melt. I asked her where Pawan was.

'You're missing Pawan a lot,' she said.

'Nothing like that . . . it's a beautiful evening; he would have enjoyed it too if he were here. Is he busy today?'

'I don't know, I didn't ask.'

'Why?'

'Arey, why would I? It's not like he is my boyfriend.'

I was surprised. Aru understood everything from the look on my face.

'Oh, that's why you keep avoiding me. You thought Pawan and I . . .' She laughed so hard that some wine from her glass spilt onto the swing. She put the glass down on the table and kept laughing.

'It was Pawan who kept telling me that you're a dear friend of his. And stressed on the word "dear" so I thought he was warning me or something.'

'And here I thought you were interested in him.'

I laughed as well. Everything was comfortable now and a sweet tension of a different kind had replaced whatever had been between us before. We both scooted towards each other. We both knew how this evening would end. The question was how we reached it and when. Till a minute ago I had been focused on the disgust I felt by meeting Aru behind Pawan's back. I would never have touched Aru, but knowing you can't touch someone is titillating. There were all sorts of conflicts; that was a story I wanted to read. So far, I had been reading an interesting story, but now it had become predictable. Now I knew all the turns it would take and all the incidents that would happen, which is tiring to go through again. It was good the day felt different; I felt weightless that day. I wanted to live to the fullest. I didn't want to break anything, just so I could go home and finish it in my writing. My writing was out of my control anyway, so I just wanted to live. Aru brought me another glass of wine. I stood up and lit a cigarette.

'Rohit. Can I call you Rohit?'

'I would love that!'

We both went to the other side of the terrace with our wine, cigarettes and ashtray and stood near the railing.

'I know how much you love mountains and rivers. You speak of them like lovers in your poems. What are you doing in this crowded city?'

'I myself couldn't figure it out. But do we really want what we believe we want?'

'Then where does the desire to live come from?'

'Maybe from our fears and the need for entertainment. We don't want to invest so much in an experience that it starts guiding our lives. We always want to leave a door or two unlatched so we can escape whenever we want to.'

'But isn't that hypocrisy? Not being completely present where one is, but also not going to the place one wants to go to.'

'Well, hypocrisy is our entertainment.'

'That's why I love acting.'

'Hmm, I never understood the allure of acting. I always see a play as the writer talking to me. Actors only seem like a medium.'

'Have you ever written plays?'

'I find writing plays very commercial. You call an audience, get the help of actors, and then all you do is exhibit what you have written.'

'Acting is therapeutic for me. You get a character to play and then you want to be that character. A web of lies is built around you, only so you can get to the honesty of the character. You find it, feel it, live it and then return home. Isn't that wonderful?'

'I've never thought of it this way.'

'In one life you get to be Rajni, Nargis, Kamla, and you are paid for it as well. I would even pay to do it.'

We were getting flirtatious in our conversation. But to what extent did we want to know each other?

Can we even know ourselves after a point? Maybe we are only trying to find ourselves more when talking to others. I always thought I knew Verma Madam, but I was so wrong. I should go back and be near my story. Suddenly I wanted to leave. I felt free today and I wanted to devote all this time to my story. I placed my glass back on the table and asked for her leave.

'There's still some wine left, but as you wish.'

'No, I certainly can't drink more, thank you.'

I shook her hand, but then we felt we should end the night with a hug at least. With much awkwardness, we opened our arms to each other. I hugged her and I realized I knew this person. I remembered the fragrance of her hair. Some people hug so warmly, that it feels like you're home. I wanted to stay like this, with the fragrance, but suddenly she started shrinking away from me. I wanted to look at her face. I put my hands on her shoulders and held her at a distance from me. She was looking downwards. Was she acting?

'You are Aru, right?'

'Why?'

'No, I asked for no reason at all.'

Aru was holding onto my shirt with a firm grip. My face was very close to hers. She closed her eyes. I started to touch her face. Her brows, nose, her lips, her cheeks . . . they were all so soft. Such beauty, like something chiselled out of stone. I placed my lips on hers and she kissed me lightly. I tasted something familiar. I felt it in my spine. I moved my face away. I didn't know what she saw in my eyes, but with a sombre tone she said, 'Good night.'

While returning home, I was trying to figure out the taste in my mouth. I licked my lips and realized it was something like cinnamon. How could it be on Aru's lips? I knew this taste, I remembered it. My tongue kept going back to my lips.

18

The next morning I stood in front of the mirror, brushing my teeth. My hands went about their usual business while my brain tried to rearrange last night's memories into some sort of order. Last night, when I came back with the taste of cinnamon still in my mouth, I switched on my computer first thing. After a long time, I wanted to pour all my happiness into my story. But I was surprised to see that my story had moved forward on its own. How? I could read only a few sentences before I had to turn my computer off. I wasn't scared, but my whole body had gone rigid. The line between my writing and my life was blurred. I started to question every one of my daily activities. Had I even met Aru? Or do I just simply go out to roam around every day and go to a cafe and think about the girl, whom I couldn't bring myself to talk to? The only thing I knew with complete certainty was that Antima had gone back to Delhi. Last night in bed I had been touching myself frantically, just to make sure it was really me who lay there on the bed. Or was I sitting on the sofa, writing about lying on the bed? Was I writing while brushing my teeth in front of the mirror too?

I stopped brushing my teeth. I splashed water on my face, just to make sure I wasn't writing this but living it. I could still taste the cinnamon. I went to my computer, but I still didn't have the courage to switch it on. I should have understood then, everything was slipping out of my control and crashing around me. So far, I have broken four glass jars, three plates and all the cups . . . I get lost in thought and things just slip from my hands. Now I had to drink tea from a steel tumbler. I had stopped writing poems because the distance between what I wrote and what I lived had been shrinking. I had no idea when I entered one of my poems and when I stepped outside my home. How dangerous is that? What one lives should always be kept separate, and what one writes should be kept shrouded in mystery, never to be let out. Our attraction to mysteries ruins almost everything. Suddenly, I had a keen desire to call up my father and tell him I wanted to get married. I couldn't live alone like this anymore. The moment this thought crossed my mind, I started laughing. I knew that other than my writing, I had no other place to hide. I took my steel tumbler full of tea and sat down in front of my computer. In my heart, I was praying for the story not to have progressed on its own. But the moment I opened the file, I knew it had gone forward. I started to read:

> The mood was poetic and now Rohit wanted to be a poet. You don't become a poet by just learning and reciting somebody else's poems, and Rohit knew this very well. Dushyant was a poet who looked like a poet . . . long

unkempt hair, a little stubble, thin and soft hands, lanky body and intoxicating eyes. Rohit had practised making his eyes look intoxicating in front of a mirror for hours. At times he would think with frustration that if people gave as much importance to kite flying as they did to poetry, he would have vanquished Dushyant by now. He would have defeated him every time, in every way. In his desperate attempts to write a poem, he would steal lines from those written by other people and try to make up his own to fill the blank pages he now carried around everywhere. But the resultant poems would end up being incomprehensible to him. Rohit sat in his room surrounded by torn and crumpled up pages: all his failed attempts at writing poetry. Dushyant would come to the village every week to meet Verma Madam and bring new poems with him. All three of them would gather on the roof, and every time Dushyant would garner all the praises from Verma Madam. After finishing his own poem, Dushyant would always ask Rohit to recite something, but he would avoid him and say, 'I'm still working on it.' Diwali holidays were near. Those were the days when you would get twenty days of leave for Diwali. This year, Verma Madam decided not to go home but to stay back to finish her thesis. Dushyant volunteered to stay with her and help her out. Rohit wanted to tell her that there was no need for him to stay. He wanted to offer his help. But he didn't think he had that kind of say. He thought he would have the right to say something if he could defeat Dushyant at least once with his poetry.

Between us is a thread worth of distance
Touch is such a meaningless word
That distance sometimes looks as long as a lifetime
At times as short as the gap between our terraces
At times the insurmountable gap of a stumble
Sometimes that distance is a shivering second
Where your hands appear dry as bone
And I spilled myself while taking water to you
You think of this as poetry
For me, it's just
a gathering of broken words and phrases like
distance, stumble, a shivering second, and thirst
If you touch it
the words will have meaning
They'll meet in poetry, uninhibited.

After Rohit finished writing the poem he was drenched in sweat. Why do people take up such difficult things? he thought. Afterwards, he kept practising reading the poem in front of the mirror. He realized it was not good enough to defeat Dushyant. To defeat Dushyant, he should write a poem on the environment, or the rising and setting of the sun or wild beasts. But it wasn't the weather that affected him, it was Verma Madam. All writing paled in front of her. He knew Dushyant wouldn't be here this weekend and Verma Madam would be alone working on her thesis. He could recite the poem to her then. He didn't take his diary with him; if Verma Madam saw his diary, she would know he had come to

read something to her. He had to keep the poem a
secret and have all the options available so that he
could perceive the situation and change his move if
necessary. He tore the page with the poem out of his
diary and put it in his pocket. When he came down
inside the house through the roof, he found Verma
Madam lying in bed, asleep. The pages of her thesis
fluttered near her face because of the fan. Rohit
collected all the pages and put a pot on them so they
wouldn't fly away. Just then she turned, and Rohit's
eye travelled directly from her deep-cut blouse to her
breasts. Her eyes were closed, and Rohit wanted to
capture this moment in his mind forever. That is when
he realized that Dushyant was a stupid poet . . . he
was near such beauty, a beauty he could touch, and
he was still writing poetry about the environment,
animals and mountains. A whimpering rose inside
Rohit; could he touch this source of Dushyant's
poetry? Because Dushyant clearly didn't care about
all this beauty. But his knees gave way at the mere
thought. He thought he would fall down. He wanted
to silently escape from there. He had just turned to
go when Verma Madam called to him.

'Rohit . . . what is it?'

'I just came to check if you needed something.'

'Come here . . . come.'

Rohit went to Verma Madam's bed. She motioned
for him to sit. She closed her eyes again and said, 'Read
me something,'

He was happy to oblige. He was about to pull the
folded page from his pocket when Verma Madam

spoke again, 'Do you remember that poem? "Tumhare Saath Rehkar"?'

'Sarveshwar Dayal Saxena?'

'Hmm.'

'Yes, I know it. Would you like to hear it?'

Rohit started reciting it as though he was taking a test. Verma Madam laughed.

'Not like that. Feel it. Imagine it was you who had written it for someone. And read it slowly, very slowly . . . I want to fall asleep while you read.'

Verma Madam said all this in a state of languor as if she were still dreaming. Then she turned her back to him. Rohit didn't understand what was happening. He pulled the page from his pocket and read the poem silently. Then he put it back. He lay down beside her. He could see her back now. His hand involuntarily moved to touch her back, but he stopped himself right before it could make contact. He slowly started to read the poem.

Being with you
I often feel
everything is close by
all paths have shortened . . .*

Rohit's hands touched Verma Madam's hair.

Rohit couldn't help but look at her bare back. It looked like the incline of a mountain, spotless and

---

* 'Tumharey Saath Rehkar' by Sarweshwar Dayal Saxena, translated by Daisy Rockwell

smooth as snow. She had probably fallen asleep. He could see each word of the poem emerging from her body. He thought Sarveshwar Dayal Saksena too might have written the poem under similar circumstances; he hadn't just written it, he'd seen it . . . lived it.

Rohit read the poem slowly. He didn't want her to wake up once the poem was finished. He pulled his hand out of her hair and touched her saree where it was tucked in her waist. His fingers trembling, he reached out and touched her back. His voice shivered and he stopped reading. He didn't pull his fingers away. She didn't move a bit. He saw goosebumps rise on her back. He didn't want her to know about the goosebumps, so he placed his hand on them and resumed the poem. This time the words poured from Rohit's mouth in all their tenderness.

He thought the goosebumps had gone because of his touch. Her skin was so smooth, but he could still feel goosebumps on his fingertips. He wanted to be rid of the goosebumps on his hand too, so he moved his hand some more on her back. There was an incline. He realized his hand was moving towards her navel. He halted on every word of the poem, the more his hand moved a little further, the more he spoke. The words were sticking inside his throat. If he tried harder, some words would break off and only half would come out of his mouth, with the other half remaining inside.

He had touched her navel. He was unable to think of anything. He realized his hand was wet; maybe he was sweating. His body was touching hers and his face was buried in her hair. He took a deep breath. He could smell the fragrance of cinnamon coming from her hair. His eyes were half closed now; maybe it was the cinnamon. He had no control over his own hand anymore. His hand was moving fast on her belly. His body was turning rigid. He was completely stuck to her now. His body was shivering, and his hips shook and trembled violently. Suddenly he felt a sharp pain in his shins. He pulled his face out of her hair and looked at his shins. That's when he saw the painting with the deer, hanging on the wall in front of him. The deer was looking directly at him. He had left the poem behind long ago. Only weird noises were coming out of Rohit's mouth now, which he hadn't heard before. His eyes were fixated on the deer. His legs turned rigid first, then went slack after some violent jerks. He realized his pants were a little wet. He lay there for a while. He felt like he had a fever. Suddenly he felt like crying. But he didn't want Verma Madam to hear him cry . . . so he held his hands tightly over his mouth and left.

If only anxiety could be washed away by pouring water over one's head. He scrubbed his body so hard, his skin broke out in angry red rashes everywhere. He stood in front of the mirror and looked at his body as if it belonged to somebody else. A pimple appeared on his face. He felt shy looking at it. A weird thought crossed his mind: he wished Verma Madam would stop ageing for a while. In a few years, he'd be the same age as her. He realized he was growing

up fast. Something inside him was changing on a
chemical level; that's why he could touch the source
of Dushyant's poetry. He could see goosebumps all
around him and as they settled down, he could see
words bursting inside them. All those words weren't
a part of his vocabulary. They felt foreign or from
another planet. He was seeing them for the first time.
Rohit would keep his diary close. Whenever he came
across such words, he would note them down. As he
wrote them, his anxiety would find a shore to land
on. One day he collected all the shored-up words and
there it was, a poem. He could hear it:

Can dreams be touched?
Will I be convinced in the morning
that I was with you in the night?
I wish you weren't a dream, but a beloved of mine.
If only I could invite you to my poetry and
keep you entangled in my words forever
I wish you were a poem
If it were so,
I'd never read that poem to anyone
But you're not a poem.
You are that mirage
wherein,
The trickster forgets his tricks
He looks for your feet in your hair
What is the extent of your being?
How should the calculation be done,
So that it doesn't leave us with a void?

Am I a void?
Can we be one in the void?

A bead of sweat dropped on his diary. He couldn't believe he had written a poem without any cuts or effort whatsoever. A task that used to feel gigantic had now turned into something easy. He read the poem and thought that for the first time in his life, he had found something he wanted. All his anxiety and nervousness had gone. He wanted to read this poem to Dushyant. Had he too become a poet like Dushyant? He turned the page and tried to write another poem. But after much effort, he couldn't manage to get a single word out. He fell on his bed and tried to feel like a poet for a long time.

The tea had gone cold in the steel tumbler. Like a robot, I got up from my writing and came back to the kitchen to heat it up. I was trying to remember when I had written this part of the story. I didn't even remember going to her house that afternoon in such fine detail. And the poetry, how could I remember what I had written then? Maybe I wasn't sleeping well. I really needed a good sleep. Waking up every night at ten past three was disorienting me. Did I fall asleep again after I woke up at ten past three and then go on to dream the rest?

I sent the new part of the story to my editor. At least he would think I was working.

19

I kept myself busy with household chores the entire day. I wanted to tire myself out. Right before I went to bed, I called my father and listened to a detailed account of him falling sick and then recovering. I felt a sense of affinity listening to him. A reassurance that I was his, a part of him, his son. After he was done, he handed the phone to Salim. Three sentences in, Salim jumped from household problems to national problems. We talked about casteism for a long time. After the call, I kept thinking about how all of us are inherently racist; it's something we have to constantly shed. We are stuck in times past, where homosexuality is still seen as a disease, a dark man is called black, a physically disabled person is called lame, and nobody finds anything wrong with it. We'd excuse ourselves by saying that only the sufferer knows his suffering best. Today's youth is more progressive. But we too were more progressive than our previous generation, and maybe our elders were more progressive than their previous generation too. It can be slow, but change is still a constant.

Some time while talking to Salim I realized that even though I corrected him on a few things, deep down I was thinking along the same lines. In reality we are all the same. When we say we've changed, it's possible that we've just learned the difference between being slightly bad and very bad. But I'm always confused about how much of a difference this has made to our lives. I had just closed my eyes when Pawan texted me, *meet me for a walk tomorrow, I need to talk to you*. I replied *okay* and put my phone away. The relations between men and women are so complicated. At first, whenever I slept with a woman, I felt like I was doing something bad. And bad things are punished by a God who looks a bit like my mother. One day everyone would find out and I would be punished badly for it. I never experienced my early relationships completely. I want to meet all the people I was in a relationship with at one time and get down on my knees to ask for forgiveness. But then I should ask Antima for forgiveness too. My offhanded *okay* to Pawan was the result of the feeling that whatever happened between me and Aru was wrong. And Pawan was the God who would be the judge of my mistakes; he would punish me. Generation after generation we haven't changed; we've just learned how to clip the talons of our inner beast.

I saw that Pawan was waiting for me. I wasn't late. He must have arrived early, yet I ran towards him.

'What happened?' I asked, instead of 'How are you?'

'Nothing . . . I was just waiting for you. Why do you always ask that, like something bad has happened?' said Pawan.

'No, you said you wanted to talk about something. So I was worried if everything was alright.' I was searching for words at this point.

'The whole world is falling apart; how can anything be okay?'

We started walking. I was getting irritated now. I wanted to ask him if he had texted me late at night just so we could take a walk. If you have something to say, say it. I suppressed my irritation and walked with him. We were both wearing face masks. Pawan pulled his mask off, took some deep breaths and put it back on.

'I heard you met Aru?' he said. I was caught off guard by his sudden question.

'Yes, just a coffee. I was in a hurry, so I left early.' Even though I tried to stop myself, I said more than I intended to.

'Yes, she told me.'

'What else did she say?'

'Nothing, just that you guys met.'

'She's a nice girl,' I said to hide my embarrassment.

'I like her a lot . . . a lot . . . a lot,' he said, looking at me. I smiled at him. The fake smile of a thief. Because I was wearing a mask, I didn't know if Pawan could understand my smile or not. I immediately pulled it down, but by then the smile was gone. Pawan had turned away. While walking I was wondering why I came to meet him; I could have avoided this easily.

'I've killed seventeen lizards in total,' said Pawan out of nowhere.

'Seventeen? That's a lot.'

'Have you ever killed one?'

'No, I like them actually.'

'You're just like the people on Facebook.'

'I'm not on Facebook.'

'I mean you're talking just like them: *oh! Lizards are so good. They help keep the house clean.* And only after I killed them, people told me that I could have simply chased them away, that they don't like the smell of eggs or ginger or onions.' Pawan shook his head with regret. He then looked at me as if I were the one who had said all this.

'But they're good suggestions.'

'Only now, after I've killed all those lizards I actually liked, are these people telling me all their home remedies. Why didn't they tell me all this before? Now I'm carrying around the guilt.'

'But how would the people on Facebook know that you'd already killed the lizards?'

'In a bout of guilt, I wrote about the incident on Facebook. Nobody said anything at the time, but then a few days ago a pregnant elephant died because someone fed her a pineapple full of firecrackers. I was sad, but when I wrote about it, condemning it in no uncertain terms, everyone started sharing my lizard story and told me that I had no right to say anything,' he said and again looked at me as though I was the one who had said it. He looked surprised as if to say, *how could you say this?*

I shrugged.

'But that wasn't it. They said because I'm a non-vegetarian, I have no right to talk about animal rights and conservation. That it's a double standard to talk against animal cruelty when there's a dead animal on my plate. I was furious. I wrote back: *what does that mean? Does that mean one can't talk about saving trees because they eat vegetables?*

I couldn't help but laugh at this. I found it very funny that Pawan was talking about all these serious things while wearing a mask.

'Did I say something wrong?' he asked.

'No, you said nothing wrong,' I said and laughed.

'Then why are you laughing?'

I stopped laughing. For a while, we walked in silence. Pawan felt guilty but he didn't want to accept it.

'Were any of the lizards pregnant?'

I don't know why I asked that. Pawan nodded in affirmation and removed his mask. I too pulled my mask below my nose to breathe. A while later, I checked the time on my phone. I thought I should leave, but then I decided to take one more round before I went. A round takes around twelve minutes. Pawan put his mask back on. We were silent for the entirety of those twelve minutes. I was about to leave when he removed his mask again, and said, 'It's a weird experience: to kill! When I killed the first lizard, I couldn't believe I could do that. At the time, I didn't have the courage to throw the body outside. But as the days passed and I killed more, a hardness crept into me. Now I kill lizards like I do any other thing: sweep the house, wipe the floors, do other household chores. I used to have a deep well of sympathy that has dried up with time. As time passes, I wonder if I killed Dushyant, too. Whenever I call myself Dushyant, I feel that there's a chappal in my hand and Pawan is lying on the floor, bloody and dead,' said Pawan, putting his mask back on.

I couldn't believe that this was the same person I had been laughing at. I wished I were Pawan, then at least I would be able to say everything as it was. I wanted to pull his mask off and see what his face looked like at that moment. Was he Dushyant or Pawan right then?

'You're very honest,' I said.

'You think so?'

'Of course.'

'Shall we?' he asked and started walking towards home.

'You're going this way?'

'I'm going to meet Aru.'

'So, this is what you wanted to discuss with me? The lizards?'

'Yes. Listen, I've written a poem about this whole affair. It's my first poem.'

'Oh, let's hear it then.'

'No, no, it's just for Aru. If she likes it, I'll show it to you as well.'

'That's good!'

'I'll have to do something to impress her.'

Whenever he spoke of Aru, Pawan turned into a child. He seemed to feel tickled every time he mentioned her. I was sad to see him leave. I felt that everything inside me was empty, like the hollow shell of a man who has donned clothes and pasted a smile on his face to hide the void inside. A strange thought emerged from this hollowness; Pawan was actually Rohit and Aru was Verma Madam, and I was Dushyant. Pawan was going to recite a poem to Verma Madam, but Dushyant had already kissed Aru. I felt like somebody had taken all the energy out of my legs. I sat down by the side of the road. I saw the bench outside the park in front of me. It was empty. I wanted to go and sit on it, but I had no energy to move. Do we live the same story our whole lives, just playing different parts? And even if a new story ventures into our lives, we give it to our old, stale characters too. We try to use many half-lived stories with their broken characters just to fill up the voids in ourselves. I composed myself and decided to finish the story about Verma Madam and get it out of my body as soon as I could so that I could experience something else. If it was possible to experience something new, that is. While going back home, I did something evil which I could see ahead of time, and I could have stopped myself, but it was the result of living in the same story over and over again that I found myself repeating the same mistakes. I texted Aru, *let's meet soon* and sent an emoji of a coffee cup along with it. She immediately texted me back, *let me know when . . . I'm game.* This I did less to get rid of the sadness residing inside me and more to assert control over the story. Tired and repentant . . . I imprisoned myself in my house.

20

Maybe my editor was right. I should write poetry instead of stories. Whenever I write a story, something feels amiss . . . like there's something more to be recorded. My characters wrest control from me. The story is no longer mine. It's been two days now since this has happened. I roam around, go to my computer and write a few lines, only to return a few hours later and delete them. I've lost control over this story. I'm just waiting for Verma Madam, for Dushyant . . . I'm a blind pawn who needs help from his characters to walk . . . only then can I do anything. My editor likes the parts of the story I sent him, he wants me to finish it soon. How do I tell him if it were up to me, I would've finished it in one day?

I was watching the monsoon go by. I didn't meet Aru because I'm a lech. I told her I was busy writing, but I would meet her soon. In the torrential rains of the last couple of days, I let myself be and did nothing. Mumbai had a near-miss with a cyclone. Some mornings were so beautiful that you could just lie in bed, mesmerised by the falling rain. Everything had been washed. The green of the trees looked like wet paint on canvas.

I remembered the early days of Delhi winters. Antima and I would wander about aimlessly. Khan Market, Mandi House, Barakhamba Road, Humayun's Tomb, Purana Qila, Jama Masjid, Gali Qasim Jaan in Ballimaran, India Habitat Centre, breakfast in an American-style diner and rajma chawal under Antima's office building. At that time, I wanted to journal everything. We were enjoying those days with utmost leisure, but I was painfully aware of them passing by as well. One day we were sitting in Café Turtle in Khan Market. I still remember it was her favourite cafe and they allowed you to smoke on the outside tables. We were reminiscing and laughing about something when Antima said, 'Do you miss Bombay?'

'Yes, I think I should go back; it's been a while.'

She didn't reply. She was staring at her coffee like she was searching for something inside the cup, and then she took a long sip.

'Listen, I need some books from the bookstore . . . do you want something?'

'I'll come with you.'

'No, it's fine, I'll be right back.'

She wanted to be alone, I think. I ordered another coffee and waited for her to come back. While waiting for her I started writing something on a napkin. At first, it looked like a poem, but then there was dialogue.

'Do you miss Bombay?' she asked.

'I miss you, sitting here in front of you, watching you drink coffee, that's what I'm missing.' She laughed at this. I got up and pressed my lips against hers. She looked around to see if anyone was looking. I kept kissing her. She pushed me away laughing.

'Arey, what are you doing? This isn't Bombay, mister. You'll leave soon but I have to live here.'

She pulled out a compact from her bag and started fixing her lipstick.

'I'll miss you falling asleep at Humayun's tomb. And the rickshaw we took in Ballimaran with the wonky wheel . . . I'll miss that wheel too. And your laughter at all my poor jokes and . . .'

'Yes, yes, got it.'

I took her hand in mine. Her nail polish had come off at the edges. I kept intertwining her fingers with mine, but they kept coming apart.

'These days feel like I'm getting to eat the cake I used to love as a child every day. I'll miss this cake.'

She then booked a return ticket for me, and we ordered more coffee.

I stopped writing, there was no more space on the napkin. It was the first time I hadn't ended up writing a poem. My story writing started in that cafe. Antima came back with some books.

'Let's go,' she said coldly.

'We can have another coffee'

'Okay, we'll book your ticket as well.'

I called for another coffee and pushed the napkin in front of her. Antima was reading what I had written, and for the first time, I could see a story forming in front of me. I can keep these days safe, not in a journal, but in stories. In the made-up reality of a story, I can say that I'm extremely in love with you and I want to see you fly. I want to lie with you, beside Humayun in the coolness of his grave. I want to kiss you at every turn. It was due to Antima that I thought about writing a story for the first time. One could find oneself with honesty there.

Can you solve the problems of your life in your own stories? Writing is like an apology to those who we know will never forgive us.

Antima put the tissue back down.

'Let's order a carrot cake too.' She was smiling.

'Of course.'

The rain had let up. Antima must be in Delhi right now. What was the weather like in Delhi? Was it raining there too?

Whenever I turned on my computer to write these days, a quiet silence engulfed me, so I stayed away from it.

There was a world of household chores to do, so I stuck to those. I would call up Salim to ask for recipes and cook new things all the time. I was not a foodie, but it made me happy to accomplish something difficult. It felt like I was doing something new. Even if momentarily, at least I was busy creating something. I went to the market and bought new cups, plates and other utensils and set them up in my kitchen. I was collecting excuses to hide my real reasons for not writing. I couldn't see them clearly. How bad would it be if my debut story collection was published without Verma Madam's story? I decided that the collection should go out without that story and wrote an email to my editor: 'You must print the other stories, I don't think I'm going to finish this one.' I kept staring at the send button like it was a declaration of failure on my part. I didn't want to fail. I closed the e-mail and sat down in front of my laptop.

21

How can one share something deeply personal? This question bothered me at times. But my whole life, I've mostly been attracted to those writers who have written what was personal to them. Reading them felt like reading about myself. The personal is so universal in their work. The question that arises then is, why did I keep guarding the personal? Maybe the thought of something private put out in the open for everyone to see was an unpleasant one. From a philosophical standpoint, I could understand that nothing was personal, that our most personal aspects aren't unique after all, we're all the same and nothing is significant. I think it was the guilt of putting myself out in the market that made me seek out other philosophies time and again. The truth was that no one anywhere had the right answers; it was just that philosophy was the sort of ointment that at least gave momentary relief from the pain. In poetry, there's no dearth of ways to hide oneself, but in a story, every dark corner seems to be illuminated as if by a lamp.

One day my father called me after reading one of my poems.

'I read your poem, the mention of Kashmir in it is dishonest.'

'Which poem?'

'You know the one I'm talking about. What do you even know about my Kashmir? Do you have any idea how difficult it was to live there? The kind of hardships we've endured? And how difficult it still is for those who are living there? It's not just azure skies, fragrances and snowy mountains; there are real devastated lives there which your falsehoods have never seen.'

This was the first time I had heard words like 'my Kashmir' coming out of my father's mouth. The biggest reason for my hatred towards my poems was my utter lack of knowledge. If I wrote a poem about my mother, then it became rather difficult to determine how much I even knew about her. When my father was unable to sleep at night, and when he sat up in his bed and stared at the darkness . . . could I write a poem about that? Never. The mere thought of being with him in the same room on one of those nights sent shivers down my spine. What would I even do? Would I turn my back to him and sleep? We're never able to do enough for anyone and we can never know anyone well enough to earn the right to write about them. Fiction seems to be the better choice because an imaginary veneer is always there to protect us. The fact that this whole world stands on a foundation of imagination is reassuring to some extent. The dense forest of our imagination is full of lies fed with the water and manure of absolute truth.

I woke up late into the night and found myself lying on the sofa. What day was it? What time was it? When I checked, it was ten minutes past three. There was a message from Antima on the phone. I turned it on. *Want to meet tomorrow?* But Antima was in Delhi, I was sure about that. I slapped myself and squealed with pain. It was a hard slap. Then I went to the bathroom and splashed water on my face . . . back to the laptop and the mobile. Where should I start? What should I write first?

Antima or the story? I texted Antima: *in the afternoon? Please. Wear a saree and if you happen to have a green thread, tie it on your right hand.* After sending the message, I pushed the phone away. I came back to the laptop, placed my fingers on the keyboard, and entered the thicket of the story:

> Vacations had started. Dushyant had come to live with Verma Madam. Rohit had not met Verma Madam since he'd seen the deer in her room. One evening, Dushyant sent him a message to join them for tea on the terrace. The invitation was good news. It came as a relief for Rohit; maybe everything was okay after all. But there was still some doubt, because the invitation had not come from Verma Madam herself. When he arrived, Dushyant welcomed him as if they were long-lost best friends. Rohit was going for a handshake, but Dushyant pulled him into a hug instead. Rohit saw that Dushyant was wearing a bindi on his forehead, which he recognized. It was Verma Madam's bindi.

Just then the phone rang with a message notification. I looked at the phone. Antima had replied: *why the green thread?*

Why had I looked at the text? I should have stayed with the story. I cursed myself and returned to the story, in which Dushyant was hugging Rohit. Just then another message chimed in. I reached out to pick up the phone when I heard her voice, 'And what am I doing there, watching Dushyant take you in his arms?'

I didn't touch the phone. I kept staring at the story instead, looking for an answer to Verma Madam's question.

'I don't know what you're doing.' I sounded pathetic.

'It was me who invited you for chai that evening, not Dushyant.'

'In my story Dushyant was the one who sent for me and that's the truth now.' I was angry. What followed was a long silence.

Seething, I picked up the phone. Antima had written: *Okay, I'll see what I can do. See you tomorrow.* I sent her a smiley and put the phone down. I was out of the story now and Verma Madam was sitting beside me.

'You say you can't write poetry anymore because you don't know people well enough, but you know exactly what I did here, so why are you trying to protect me?'

'I'm not protecting anyone.'

'But you are.'

'No.' I was adamant.

'I pinched you and asked you why you hadn't recited the whole poem that day. I'd been listening so affectionately, why had you left midway? Didn't I?'

'Yes.'

'Then why are you scared of writing it?'

'I'm not scared.'

'You're trying to avoid it because if you write truthfully about me then the image you have of me in your mind will shatter. All of you men have the same problem! You want the women out there to be promiscuous, except for the ones who come into your life; they should be pure, virgin goddesses.'

'It's nothing like that! I was about to come to it. I mean it has to be written.'

'You can write about me. You remember, right, what I told you?'

I stayed quiet. I still remember that evening . . .

The sky had taken a golden hue, and a pigeon was perched near Verma Madam. Rohit had come to recite a poem to her, and she was staring at the pigeon. After some time, the pigeon flew over and sat on Rohit's terrace. Verma Madam made Rohit sit beside her. When Rohit read out his poem to her, she kissed him on the cheeks and placed her bindi on his forehead. It was the first time that Verma Madam had enjoyed Rohit's writing so much. She said, 'Listen, you can write about me . . . in any manner you see fit . . . you don't need to hide me or hide from me.'

How can I forget that evening when I had learnt that a poem is only complete when the listener starts to see themselves in it?

'You tore out that poem from your diary and gave it to me. Remember?' Verma Madam spoke in a whisper.

'Yes.'

'Do you remember it?'

'How can I not remember it? I consider it to be my first poem, just as I think of Dushyant as my first . . .'

I could not finish the sentence.

'Recite it for me.'

I could feel Verma Madam's warm breath on my neck. I couldn't refuse and started to recite the poem. I was surprised I remembered the entire thing word for word:

When you ask me to look at you
Who am I looking at?
When a mirror is in front of me,
I see your bindi on my face
Maybe the bindi is actually on the mirror
When I touch my face
A hint of cinnamon lingers on my hands
You were here just now, somewhere nearby
But you had no bindi
I shake my clothes before putting them on, searching for it
Strangeness falls from them
Without you, everything comes shrouded in futility
You untie your hair, and I wordlessly stare at you
The significance of my existence,
Just like your bindi,
Is entangled in your hair.
By the time I reach out to touch it,
It vanishes in the thick braid of relationships
Wherever I go,
It feels like you had just left
When I talk to others
I see your bindi everywhere.
In my quest to gather your every whisper

I search for you even when you're with me
Who am I looking at,
When you ask me to look at you?

A long silence followed. A pigeon had entered the kitchen and forgotten the way out. It kept slamming into a windowpane. The fool didn't understand it was glass. A window was open right next to the glass, but in its attempts to get out, it kept flying into the glass. I was having difficulty breathing. I thought of running to the kitchen and opening the window. But I came back to the story.

'Don't do this.'

I didn't listen to what Verma Madam said.

'You're only doing this to justify your actions.'

I ignored what she said and moved the story forward . . .

After hugging Dushyant, Rohit went near Verma Madam. Verma Madam had no bindi on her forehead.

'Good evening, Madam!'

'Come here . . .' Verma Madam pinched his waist and asked, 'Why didn't you recite that poem completely yesterday? I was listening so affectionately, why did you leave halfway?'

When Verma Madam started laughing, Dushyant said, 'Arey wah! Which poem was it? I would like to hear it too.'

'Oh you must . . . Rohit, you must recite Sarveshwar Ji's poem to him too, the same way you recited it to me.'

Verma Madam couldn't control her laughter now and Rohit's face had turned red. Dushyant on the other hand had no idea what was going on.

'Hey, how exactly did you recite it? I'd love to know.'

Verma Madam realized that Rohit was getting uncomfortable. She tried to manoeuvre the conversation in a different direction.

'Dushyant has written such a beautiful poem . . . I want you to hear it . . .'

'I just read it out to you . . . I'll read it to him later.'

'Please, Dushyant.' Verma Madam held Dushyant's hand and pulled him towards her.

'Okay okay.'

Dushyant cleared his throat and looked at Verma Madam as if the poem were written on her face. Jealousy was a pigeon, painfully struggling to get out from somewhere inside Rohit. He felt as if he was somewhere far away from Verma Madam . . . standing at the bottom of a deep dry well listening to the poem. Each and every word of the poem echoed inside him. Dushyant was reciting the poem in a baritone . . .

When you ask me to look at you
who am I looking at?

Dushyant recited the complete poem. When he was done, Verma Madam kissed him. Dushyant plucked the bindi from his forehead and placed it back on her forehead and kissed her back. Verma Madam was looking at Rohit as Dushyant kissed her. Rohit started to look around for the pigeon that usually fluttered nearby but couldn't be found anywhere now that it was needed the most. But Rohit could feel its fluttering everywhere inside him.

I took a deep breath after writing this. I knew Verma Madam would say something about what I had written. I kept waiting but there was no sound whatsoever.

'I can make changes to it if you want?'

My sentence hung in the air, never reaching its close.

22

I got up and went to the kitchen. I opened the kitchen window but there was no pigeon there. So I went back to the bed with the bird's restlessness instead. I wanted to at least sleep for an hour before dawn. I lay there with my eyes closed but a question kept haunting me: was I exacting revenge on my childhood? If not at my childhood, then was I taking revenge on Verma Madam or was I angry with myself . . . maybe not with the entirety of my being, but just the way I was at this moment . . . no, it was all my failures that I wanted to exact revenge on, and on the breathtakingly beautiful Dushyant. I don't know who. How many people can be responsible for something? Why did I want to ruin everything I had forever dreamt of having, again and again?

I still remember thinking about living with Verma Madam while I waited for her on my terrace. If not her, then somebody like her. Dreams of building a home, of travelling far away in a train, of love, of sharing happy moments, of a simple life, where life is laid out in front of you like a long, empty path and at every turn there's a cot under a peepal tree to rest. I wanted to lead a simple life with her, have a simple job, own a small house, have small problems and the momentary joy that comes from solving such problems . . . that was all. And to be invisible in this simple life, so that no one could see us. Now writing about it feels vain and pretentious. Something that was true at one point in your life doesn't hold up at another time. Looking back, it's hard to believe that at some point that was the truth we lived. When did things become this difficult? When did our lived experiences start dissolving in front of our eyes? When did the previous steps start to disappear as we moved up ahead? Can one change things by writing them into a story? Or would I drop this story upon encountering another old difficulty?

The night had crossed into the morning. I was asleep for a long time. Sleep was keeping me bound to the bed. What day was it? What time was it? If you check the time, your brain skips over from the world of dreams to this convoluted present. But today I stayed in my bed. Everything was dark outside despite the day. Crows cawing and other bird songs were lost in their clamour. Every leaf on every tree was still. It looked like it was about to rain. Rain always enters the scene so dramatically. It creates an atmosphere, alerting people with its warning signs—go inside your houses, sit around your balconies and windows, and then everything goes quiet and dark and suddenly it comes pouring down.

It had been the rainy season when my mother passed away. The house had felt strange and eerie, like somebody had taken apart every bit of normal between me and my father. We would lie about the house like someone had taken the stuffing out of us. We stared at each other, not knowing how to comfort one another.

It was with difficulty that I reached my village from Mumbai in torrential rains. Everyone in the village kept telling me that I'd have to take care of my father now as if he had been crippled . . . he didn't like that one bit. He would save me from our relatives again and again. *If you have something to do in Mumbai, then you should go, I'll manage everything here,* he had said. I couldn't bear to look at my father doing everything on his own in that house and brought him to Mumbai. But in Mumbai, it did seem like he had lost his limbs. I had taken him away from all his friends. His afternoons with Raghu Kiranewala, the debates he had with other old men in the park in the evenings and his room, which he had ruled for years, I had taken away everything. I realized my mistake very soon and went to drop him back.

A few days ago, I related a dream I had about Kashmir to my father. I could feel the energy coursing through him as he listened. He was so happy that he began telling me things about Kashmir that were related to my dream. Maybe it's because of this lockdown that I could gather enough courage to relate my dream about Kashmir to him in its entirety. Now that dream is an important part of my relationship with my father. He would also tell me stories from his time in Kashmir, but only tiny ones. They would just be only long enough that I couldn't ask any questions. I wanted to say to him that dreams too are imaginary, just like my stories and poems but he listened to each and every one of my dreams as if I had lived them at some point in time. He would start to look for the stories and the characters behind those dreams in real life.

One time, I dreamt that I was sitting on a horse and climbing the hills of Pahalgam. I had a mobile phone in my hand, and I was taking pictures of my father who was wearing a red sweater. Then my father ran towards a dhaba and sat down to have some rajma chawal. The scene then shifted to a dhaba in Banihal, and we were sitting together eating piping hot rajma chawal. Our bus was about to leave but because the food was extremely hot, I couldn't eat it fast enough. My father started to run with me with the plate in his hands. As we ran, he fed me spoonful after spoonful. We somehow boarded the bus, which had started moving. By the time I realized that we were on the wrong bus, we had come a long way, and my father was already asleep. I couldn't tell him that the bus was going in the wrong direction.

Once he heard that one, he couldn't stop laughing.

'Why is Ma not there in any of these dreams?' I asked him.

'Because she considered Kashmir a foreign country.'

'Really?'

'Yes, she always thought we lived abroad, and she would call Mumbai a dream.'

'A dream.'

'When you left for Mumbai, I would taunt her, *see, your husband is a foreigner and your son is lost in a dream. Now you must decide where you belong.*'

'What did Ma say to that?'

My father didn't say anything. He then made an excuse and hung up.

That's when I saw a lizard enter my house via the upper corner of the door. It must have moved only ten paces when it stopped. Maybe it realized that somebody was watching it. I texted Pawan: *A lizard has just entered my room.* It had stopped in the space between the ceiling and the wall. I rolled over on my bed and it too took a few steps. When I sat up it ran towards the window. I thought if it went out the window, it might be in danger. I sat still on the bed, and it stayed still where it was. Had the news of the seventeen murders spread among the lizards? How do I tell them that I'm not Pawan? We human beings have numerous petty fears whereas animals have only one, death. I slowly tiptoed out of the room . . . later, when I checked, the lizard was no longer there.

23

When I went to the other room, my computer was still on. I closed it and went to the kitchen to make chai. I checked my phone; Pawan had read the message but hadn't replied. That was weird. I thought I would check up on the story. What had I written last night? But I was still tired. I decided I would check it after chai. That's the difference between truth and lies. Lies have a network of lanes, where we can hide for hours, but the truth is like a straight road with not even a tree to provide shade from the sun. There are no destinations at the end of a lie, but with truth, we are certain to reach home in the end. Last night, I wandered in the lanes of lies. I stubbornly decided that the story would contain all these lies, even if I couldn't reach home in the end.

The rain wasn't ready to fall yet. The air was heavy around me. I thought about calling my father, but I didn't have a dream about Kashmir to tell him. I called anyway and listened to him talk about his day. He was complaining about Salim; he had stopped giving him the one cup of sweet tea like he used to. Salim was proving to be a better son. My father had gotten Salim a job in the L.I.C. office. He didn't have to come back to my father's house anymore, but he is Salim, not Rohit. Whenever I talk to Salim, there's an underlying guilt in my voice, which Salim graciously ignores. When I disconnected the call, I saw that Antima had texted me: *I'll be there in five minutes.* I read the message and then looked around at my house, which was in disarray. A current ran through my body. I picked up all the clothes and stuffed them inside the almirah, picked up a broom and cleaned the outer room, changed the sheets on the bed, washed all the dirty utensils and put them back in their places, wiped the kitchen floor and cleaned the gas stove. I saw that there were cobwebs in the corners, but if I cleaned them, I'd have to sweep the floor again, so I let them be. When I heard the bell ring, I saw a lizard run above the door frame. I shooed it away and opened the door. The moment I opened it, Antima threw her purse on the sofa and ran towards the bathroom. I cursed myself for forgetting to clean it.

'Sorry, the bathroom might be a bit dirty, are you okay?' I called from outside but received no reply. Suddenly I had a strange thought. Was this happening for real? Did Antima really come to my house? Or was I writing that she had arrived and ran towards the bathroom? I wanted to hit myself, but it was better to check for her purse in the other room. I saw that it was still on the sofa. So, she was in the bathroom, and all this was really happening. I sat down on the sofa, opened my computer and started looking at my story. I was surprised. The story had moved forward. How could it progress? Just then Antima came out.

'It's so difficult to pee in a saree. Were you saying something?' she asked.

I stared at her in bewilderment.

'What happened?' she asked, sitting beside me.

'I don't know what's going on with me.'

'What's going on?'

'Am I going crazy? Everything is a mess.'

'Rohit, don't scare me, okay? Do you have Covid?'

'No . . . no . . . I'm unable to write, but my story keeps progressing.'

Antima laughed.

'What do you mean?' she asked while trying to suppress her laughter.

'I mean, maybe I'm not the one writing?'

'Then who is? I think either you aren't able to bear the lockdown, or you're enjoying it a lot.'

I was silent. How could I tell her that Verma Madam was the one doing the writing? The same Verma Madam whom she resembled in that moment. I saw that Antima had tied a thin strip of green cloth around her wrist. I touched the strip. Antima blushed.

'Where was I supposed to find a green thread? I used whatever I had.'

'You look really beautiful,' I said.

But she changed the topic.

'Good thing I brought some sarees from Delhi as well, for meetings and such.'

She stood up and showed me her saree. I moved closer to her.

'You're here, right?' The words escaped my mouth as I touched her sari. She pinched me and I cried out in pain.

Antima laughed but the story had started to move inside me.
That night on the terrace, what had happened with Verma
Madam and what hadn't? Antima was in a really good mood,
and I didn't have the heart to ask her if I could go and write.
We went to the kitchen. She had brought ground coffee with
her. She put two cups of it in my Moka pot and put it on my
stove. After a minute I saw she had a cloth in her hand and
was wiping my kitchen clean.

'Arey, I just cleaned it.'

She stared daggers at me. I went and stood silently in
a corner. She took the jars of tea powder and sugar off the
shelf and found weeks' worth of oil collecting and drying
under them. I picked up another piece of cloth and went
to help her.

'Listen, either you do it yourself or let me. I can't tolerate
this much dirt. It'll be done by the time coffee is ready.'

I backed away again and leaned against the almirah.

'I have some bad news,' I said.

'Oh no . . . please, the whole world is full of bad news
right now. I don't want to hear.'

'Okay.'

She kept cleaning for a while but then she stopped and
asked, 'Is everything okay at your home?'

'Arey, not that kind of bad news.'

She resumed cleaning but then she couldn't bear it
anymore.

'Okay, tell me!'

'You remember your favourite bookstore in Khan
Market?'

'Circle?'

'Yeah, that's closed. Forever.'

Antima threw the cloth down on the floor. She exhaled
and put both her hands on the kitchen platform before
hanging her head between her shoulders. I had never seen
Antima without books. According to her, if you live without
books, you're only living one-fourth of your life. She was sad.
Her gloom spread from the rest of the cleaning to the coffee
making and then drinking on the balcony.

'Again, bad timing . . . you were in such a good mood
and I . . . I shouldn't have told you this. At least not now.'

'I'm fine.'

She opened her purse and took out a napkin to wipe her
tears away.

'I bought the English translation of your poems there.'

'You kept pestering the bookstore owner about that book.
He had to stock it for you.'

'It was such a bad translation.'

'The poems were average only.'

'But in Hindi, . . . let it be, you talk about your poetry the
way people talk about bad relationships.'

We finished the rest of the coffee in silence.

'I want to lie down,' she said, and we moved towards the
bedroom.

'I should have been the one to translate your poems,
you know!'

'You didn't have the time then. Should I turn on the AC?'

'No, the fan is okay.'

Antima fell on the bed like she had had a tiring day of
running errands. Our friendship had reached a place where
we could feel at home with each other's touch. Maybe this
is the last stage of love after traversing all the good and bad,
where you can feel at home just by touching the other person.

The minute she closed her eyes, the lines from her forehead disappeared. Antima wanted to hold onto the past the way she held onto her handkerchief. Whenever she went to see her parents in the mountains, she cried upon seeing them. She couldn't bear the fact that they were ageing. Even now, while asleep, she held me tight. When her grip loosened, I moved away and extracted her handkerchief from her fist and put it on the table. I caressed her forehead, moving my fingers through her hair and massaged the scalp gently. I had let the old things go, but whenever Antima mentioned them, I realized that I had kept the past closer than I thought. But I didn't let the shadows from the past show on my face. I had created some sort of a mirage inside . . . whatever old was buried in me was so deeply buried that it was almost lost. It was only writing that gave me permission to open each and every door. It was in writing that everything buried started to float to the surface. That's why my own writing scares me.

Antima looked so beautiful as she slept. I was always haunted by guilt because of the pain she'd gone through because of me. There's one thing that's still a part of our relationship . . . her sleep. She would always sleep the deepest near me. That's what love is, somebody's mere presence helps you sleep well.

Whenever I went to Delhi for some work, she would take the keys to my hotel room from me. When I returned to my room, I would find her sleeping peacefully on the bed. Sometimes I had to sleep on the sofa.

Antima took my hand, put it on her cheek and turned to the other side. For a while I sat beside her, trying not to move. I could still see the green cloth on her wrist. Antima is such a good friend that she can never hurt me like a story. For that kind of pain, I'd have to go back to the story. I couldn't resolve it from the outside. I pulled my hand away slowly and came to sit in front of my computer.

As I read the story, I realized Verma Madam had pulled me out of the lies and thrown me on the road straight to the truth. What I had written last night had changed. I was angry. But the story had moved forward, and I had to finish reading it.

24

Vacation had started and Dushyant had come to live with Verma Madam. Rohit had not seen her since the afternoon he'd seen the deer in her room. Verma Madam had sent for him many times, but every time he told his mother he had lots of homework to finish. Rohit only went to the river in the afternoons, where he would swim in it for hours on the pretext of looking for coins. That was the place he felt the safest. The world of fear and guilt could not enter the water.

One evening he heard Verma Madam talking to his mother just outside the door to his room. Before he could prepare himself, his mother had opened the door.

'See, he's still sitting in bed. He never wants to leave.'

This was the first time that Verma Madam had ever come inside his room. Rohit hid his face in his diary.

'What happened? Why are you hiding your face like this?'

Verma Madam sat down on the chair while Ma stood.

'I don't know what homework he's doing all the time. It's your influence; he was never this studious before.'

'Oh, you're studying? Then that's okay,' joked Verma Madam.

'Would you like some tea?'

'No thank you, I've already made tea for him. We'll take it on the terrace. Shall we?'

'No, I'm a little busy,' replied Rohit.

'You try and figure out what's wrong with him; I need to go. His father must be waiting for his tea.'

Rohit stopped pretending to read after Ma left. Verma Madam came over and pinched him.

'Why didn't you read the rest of that poem? I was listening so lovingly; why did you run away halfway?'

Rohit couldn't stop himself from laughing. He didn't know if the laughter was from shame or because she had pinched him. Verma Madam was smiling.

'Rohit, the age you're at right now is wonderful. If I were in your place, I would have behaved exactly the same way. Look, I'm your friend, so you don't need to hide from me.'

Verma Madam was sitting too close to him. Rohit's ears were turning red. He was worried his mother would come back. He scooted away from her and started looking at his diary again.

'So, we aren't friends anymore? Okay then.'

She stood up to leave.

'We're good friends,' replied Rohit.

'That's not how you keep a friendship with someone. I've come to take you with me, but you aren't even talking to me.'

For the first time, Rohit looked up at her.

'I've written something.'

Rohit tore a page from his diary and handed it to her. Verma Madam sat beside him and started reading the poem. Rohit could smell the cinnamon now. He took a deep breath and started to look surreptitiously at her neck. He thought that her neck resembled a deer's. He spotted a mole between her neck and her shoulder. He thought that this might be a new mole. He had never seen it before. After she was done reading the poem, Verma Madam smiled at him and then kissed him on the cheeks. Before Rohit could understand what was happening, she took him by the hand and led him up to the terrace. Dushyant was waiting for them there.

'You took so long. The tea must have gone cold,' said Dushyant when he saw them coming.

'Forget about the tea, read this . . . you're going to love it.'

Verma Madam handed the page to Dushyant.

'You wrote this?' asked Dushyant.

'Yes.' Rohit felt weightless.

'It's your poem, you must read it.'

'No, you read better than I do,' said Rohit sheepishly.

'Okay.'

Verma Madam pulled Rohit closer and stuck her bindi on his forehead. Dushyant cleared his throat and looked at Rohit for permission to begin.

When you ask me to look at you
Who am I looking at?
When there's a mirror in front of me,
I see your bindi on my face
Maybe the bindi is actually on the mirror
When I touch my face
A hint of cinnamon lingers on my hands . . .

Rohit was really happy with his poems being read out this way. He was happy with Verma Madam's presence, standing so close to her and with the sensation that her kiss had left on his cheek. He was happy with Dushyant's baritone, which had given his poem a deeper meaning. He was happy with the pigeon that wasn't there. He was happy that his terrace was so close to Verma Madam's. He was extremely happy at that moment.

After he was done reading the poem, Dushyant came up to Rohit and said, 'Hi, have we met before?' He laughed and hugged him.

'Did you like it?' he asked shyly.

'It has just begun, my friend. We'll be hearing more of your poems, but it's also important to heat up the tea.'

And with that, he went downstairs with the teapot.

'You see, a poet likes your poem,' said Verma Madam.

'Dushyant has such a beautiful voice. The poem became much more beautiful in his voice. It felt like it was he who had written the poem.'

'It's a beautiful poem,' said Verma Madam.

'So will it be this painful every time I write a poem?' asked Rohit, tucking the piece of paper into his pocket.

'Giving birth to anything is painful. Even seeds have to break open beneath the earth, only then will a beautiful tree emerge. Forget about it . . . tell me, what do you want in exchange for writing such a beautiful poem?'

He wanted everything but he had no words to express that. He wished that at this moment he had a bouquet of flowers, and he could tear each and every petal off of every flower. He wanted to destroy the flowers. He wanted to tear this moment in two, with him and Verma Madam on one side, so that Dushyant who had gone downstairs to heat the tea, would never be able to reach them. He wished for Verma Madam to be a painting of a deer that he could stick to the wall in his room forever. He wanted to kiss her. He wanted to live inside her, sliding on her back and entering through her navel. But more than all that he wanted to tell her that he didn't want to write poetry anymore. He didn't like the place poetry came from. But all the same, he also wanted to write a poem about it all, and then tear it up, burn it, bury it . . . so, no one would know of its existence.

'I don't need anything,' said Rohit.

'You need some tea at least,' called out Dushyant as he returned with a teapot of hot tea.

Dushyant kept talking about the poem while drinking his tea. He saw a lot of potential in Rohit.

'You know in the beginning I could write poems about anything. I saw poetry in everything. What I felt deep inside me kept taking the shape of words day and night. In my plate of food, in the market, in the coins that fell from someone else's pocket, in the morning, during sleepless nights . . . and they wouldn't stop haunting me until I wrote them all down. Listening to your poem reminded me of those innocent days.'

Rohit saw that Dushyant's face was gentle and kind, and he smiled with his eyes. *How did he know what happened to me?* thought Rohit.

'Does that still happen to you?'

'I wish. Now everything is turned on its head. Now I wait for ages . . . I have to chase after words now. Sometimes I see them, but then they vanish the minute I touch them.'

'Why do you write poetry then?' asked Rohit innocently. *Both of them laughed.*

'Did I ask something wrong?' Rohit was embarrassed.

'No, of course not,' Dushyant said. 'It's an important question the answer to which isn't always apparent. I can guess why I still write but I can't give you any one concrete reason.'

'I don't want to write poems.'

Dushyant was silent. He finished his tea and watched the pigeon flying above him in the sky. Verma Madam plucked the bindi from Rohit's face and put it back on her forehead.

'There was a time when you found Hindi a tedious subject, and now you're writing poems. I'm content with this change, since you've read so many poems to me! I was so surprised, as there were many poets about whom I heard from you for the first time,' said Verma Madam.

'But I didn't understand most of them,' replied Rohit.

'There are new upheavals inside you and you're honest about them. I understand that you don't want to write poetry,' said Dushyant slowly and cautiously as if weighing every word and speaking to himself.

'No, you can't understand.'

Rohit was adamant. Dushyant hurriedly went downstairs and returned with a notebook and a pen. He opened it to a blank page and gave it to Rohit.

'Now write what you don't want to write. Whatever words come to your mind, just put them down as is.'

'I don't want to write.' Rohit tried to return the pen.

'Not poetry, write whatever comes to your mind.'

'Arey, if he doesn't want to write, don't force him,' Verma Madam intervened.

'Okay, fine,' Dushyant said.

The night had swallowed the remaining evening light. Rohit was frozen in place. He could only see the blank page and the pen beside it. Verma Madam picked up the empty teapot and the cups and headed downstairs.

'I'm going to do some work. Dushyant, are you coming?'

'I'll be there soon.'

Dushyant picked up the pen and the notebook.

'Listen, don't think too much about it. Write whenever you feel like it.'

When Dushyant was about to get up, Rohit took the notebook from him. Dushyant tried to take it back, but Rohit didn't let him. He asked him for the pen. Dushyant reluctantly gave it to him and left.

When Rohit was about to touch the pen to the paper, he realized that his hands were shaking. Other than the page in front of him, everything else was engulfed in darkness. Rohit's hair was fluttering in the soft breeze. There was no one on the terrace except for him. Rohit brought the blank page so close to his eyes that everything looked white. He felt as if he was hiding underwater in a river, but instead of fish, words floated around him. He saw the words swimming near him. The fish now perched on his shoulders, his hands and his knees.

I stopped reading. I was no longer questioning who had written this. My question was why it was being written at all. Why had Verma Madam left? And Dushyant? No, I don't want to go there. I just wanted to keep the story on this side of the river. There's tremendous pain on the other side and I was trying to save myself from that. But was it possible to avoid any more? I'd just started reading further when I remembered that Antima was asleep inside. When I went to check on her she was in a deep slumber. Her saree was draped haphazardly. I went and lay down beside her. I had a deep desire to turn her towards me and tell her how much I loved her. I was trying to avoid going to the other side of the river; I wanted Antima to keep me here. It was so peaceful to just lie beside her. Maybe it's at such peaceful moments that you find yourself alone and you realize that this is what you wanted the whole time. I put a hand on Antima's shoulder and turned her towards me. She stretched. Looking at her face felt like staring into a mirror. She looked so solemn, I was afraid the mirror would shatter the moment I touched her. I wanted to ask her, 'Are you dreaming?' Where must she be wandering right now? We can't ever completely know anyone. I wanted to be a part of these dreams she was having, with a smile on her lips and not a line of worry on her forehead. Then I had a keen desire to wake her up, to break the piety of the moment, push her back into the deep loneliness that she had worked so hard to climb out of. When you love someone, you want to see them swimming in a sea of unfathomable joy. When she woke up, I'd ask her what dream she had. Where was she? What brought this smile to her face? And then I'd try to make that dream come true.

25

After some time, Dushyant came back upstairs to smoke and saw that Rohit was still there.

'You're still here? What happened? Is everything okay?'

Dushyant sat beside him. He saw that Rohit was still holding the notebook, but that the page was not blank anymore.

'Read it to me,' he said.

Rohit turned the notebook towards him. Dushyant slid the unlit cigarette back into his pocket and took the notebook.

Whenever I look into a mirror,
The man on the other side pities me
He sees what I cannot
Have you ever touched that which is life? he asks
I lift my hand to do so
And just before my fingers reach it, it changes

I'm taken aback, I don't know it anymore
It's a deer now, clad in a saree, with a deep navel
I want to touch it
The nearer I go, the more it changes
I feel myself soaking through
And in between all the changes, I see life
I try my best to touch it,
When suddenly glass shatters all around me.

Dushyant had muttered the poem to himself, instead of reading it aloud. When Dushyant looked up at him afterwards, Rohit was crying. His tears came from somewhere deep within him. Dushyant took his hand, pulled him near and hugged him. Rohit was overwhelmed by the gesture and collapsed into him. He let himself go in his arms as if he'd been holding himself up for a long time. Dushyant rubbed his back.

'It's beautifully written,' he whispered to Rohit, who still clung to his chest.

'I don't want to write.'

Rohit could barely get the words out. Dushyant took his face in his hands and said, 'You've done a wonderful job. You must save whatever's inside, you mustn't let all of it go, hold it in, then put it in your writing. Yours is an exciting new voice and I wish to hear more of it.'

Rohit's tears wouldn't stop. His face was very close to Dushyant's. Rohit didn't want to cry, he was trying his best to stop, but he teared up again and again. He wanted to wipe his tears away, but he was holding onto Dushyant's shirt. He thought that if he let go, all would be lost. To him, it felt like Dushyant was drowning. Suddenly he felt as though a flock of pigeons were flying behind Dushyant. And in front of him galloped the same deer, which was still on Verma Madam's wall. He gazed at Dushyant's lips. He saw yellow and orange flowers floating around on his lips. He came close to the petals and slowly started to pick them with his lips. He could feel the softness of each and every petal. The petals dissolved in his mouth like lumps of sugar the moment they touched his lips. The more petals he touched, the more flowers he could see emerging from Dushyant's mouth. The colours and the fragrance of these flowers were so intoxicating, his eyes were closing. He wanted to tell Dushyant that he wished to fall into a deep slumber, but he was also very hungry. He had a hunger for those petals, something he realized only after he had tasted them. He was devouring them one after another.

When Verma Madam came upstairs looking for Dushyant, she saw them and froze in place. She felt she was witnessing the creation of a poem. Amidst the darkness, in the face of the storm, a flame dances, defiant.

On the riverbank, near the fort, under the peepal tree, Dushyant and Rohit lay together. Sunlight filtered through the leaves and fell on their naked bodies. Their bodies seemed to glow in that light.

'There's a pattern everywhere, and all of us are connected to it. A huge work of art; we're mere brush strokes. And the thing about this work of art is that it's constantly changing. You, with your colour and your patterns, are only a part of this artwork for a short while. After a while, a new stroke of the brush will cover you with a new colour, and you will be buried deep inside. And that's our only contribution,' said Dushyant. Rohit could visualise the ever-changing formations of this pattern.

These days Rohit lived more and more inside his head. Verma Madam was busy finishing her thesis, but Dushyant had lots of time. Most of his time was spent with Rohit. The two of them would head to the river in the afternoons; diving for coins was their favourite activity. Rohit was used to the river, he could hold his breath and stay underwater for a long time, but Dushyant couldn't stay under for long. Often, when Dushyant came up to breathe, he had to wait for Rohit so long that he worried that he might have drowned. Rohit would resurface a moment later and laugh at him for worrying. Afterwards, they would sit in their beloved place, under the peepal tree behind the ramparts on the riverbank and count the money they had collected. Rohit would mostly win, but their game had gone beyond mere wins and losses. Though a long time had passed, their relationship was still held together by poetry. In some beautiful moments, Rohit would see flower petals blooming from Dushyant's lips and would readily pick them with his own . . .

Joy is a stranger
No matter how much love you give it
It won't lose its otherness
If we are patient,

A tiny bird will come and sit near us
That is joy
But it can't stay forever
Life is momentary, we arrive and we fly away
The joy is in picking out tiny moments in between
Everything after is imaginary
Everything before is a mirage
Everything is here, in this made-up world
Lying all around us
Trying to capture the happiness from all this
Is our blindness
Can you see it?

Dushyant was lying down when he read this poem aloud. Rohit sat looking towards the far bank of the river.

'When did you write this?'

'Last night,' Dushyant said.

'And for whom?'

'You shouldn't ask a writer such questions. The poem is written for anyone who likes it.'

'When we talk it feels like you're very close to me, but then sometimes you just push me away.'

'How was the poem?'

'See you did it again . . . you just pushed me away,' said Rohit, lying down next to him.

'It was wonderful,' he whispered.

Rohit's dreams were shaded with different hues these days. And all those colours converged to create a painting in which he saw himself turning into a deer. Maybe it was the deer's curse that it had to watch

Dushyant and Verma Madam sleep together every day. Sometimes Rohit would touch Dushyant's hands and think about how these hands had touched Verma Madam everywhere the night before, and pangs of jealousy would rise inside him, but curiosity took root as well; he wished he could ask Dushyant what places on Verma Madam's body his hands had touched the night before. He would reprimand himself again and again . . . where was he going with this? What were these lanes he was itching to take and what was he searching for?

One evening, the three of them were having tea on the roof. Dushyant and Verma Madam were sitting together, side by side. Rohit sat at some distance with his tea and biscuits. Rohit loved seeing them together, but he was also pained every time Verma Madam held Dushyant's hand, or Dushyant whispered something in her ear and both of them laughed. Sometimes he couldn't understand which one he envied.

'I want to read a poem,' said Rohit.

'Oh yes, please,' said Dushyant and he scooted near Rohit. Dushyant was tranquil. He had love for everyone and a strange attraction for everything beautiful in the world.

If I'm put somewhere,
I wish to lie there, still
Until someone else touches me
I wish for a quiet stillness
Until I've gone through everything
If you come, come home

Else let me be, till I cease to exist
If you come near, there shouldn't be a breath's worth
of space
Or just leave, like people do, till they're nothing left
but ashes
I'm sick of the monotony of every new effort
I just wish to drown and stay under . . .
till I become the river.

After Rohit was done reading the poem, he saw Dushyant sitting with his head lowered, as if pondering something. A weird uneasiness had spread between the three of them.

'Oh wow, that was such a beautiful poem,' said Verma Madam.

'It's absolutely terrible. Why are you writing like this? What happened? Why do you have to write a poem, while thinking of it like a poem? Either don't write or write what you . . . you . . . I don't know . . . you . . .'

Dushyant felt that he had said too much, he stood up without finishing his sentence and went to stand in a corner of the roof. Rohit crumpled up the paper on which he had written the poem and hid it in his fist.

'Dushyant, it's such a good poem. What's wrong with you? And he is trying, he'll write many kinds of poems. You shouldn't have said that.'

Dushyant walked back to Rohit, snatched the poem from his hand and tore it to pieces right in front of him. 'I'm doing this because once when I had written such a terrible poem, nobody threw it away and I still regret it.'

The three of them belonged to three different worlds. All of them had come out of their lanes to meet at this intersection. It was obvious there would be friction, and someone would get hurt by the resultant sparks. Rohit was the one hurting here. He was at that age where every little change was unbearable and yet had to be endured. Every time he felt the pangs of pain rise, he wanted to hide from everyone. Although one could hide oneself in poetry, the poem that Dushyant expected from him required the poet to be naked and vulnerable whereas Rohit wrote with the fear of being caught naked.

Near the fort, by the riverside, under the peepal tree, in some beautiful moments, when Rohit saw the flower petals emerging from Dushyant's lips, he couldn't muster enough courage to pluck them. Whenever Rohit found himself near him, Dushyant turned away from him. When, on some afternoons, in a bid to see Verma Madam, Rohit made his way to her room, he found it locked from the inside. Standing there he could hear Dushyant and Verma Madam's laughter. He could not get rid of the scenes that crept into his mind, no matter how vigorously he shook his head. Sitting alone in his room with those scenes, he wanted to write, but he was tired of this habit. He didn't want to make poetry out of every upheaval; be it the evening tea or swimming in the river, he always found himself at a distance from those two. Verma Madam was truly busy, but even after spending the whole day with him,

Dushyant seemed far away. The day was coming to an end and the time when Dushyant would have to leave was coming closer too. Rohit didn't just want to spend as much time as possible with him, but he actually wanted to be his. He wanted to enter his very being, and Dushyant maintaining a distance was unbearable for him.

One day near the fort, by the riverside, under the peepal tree, Rohit spotted some flower petals on Dushyant's lips. He handed Dushyant a piece of paper. Dushyant sat up as if he had been eagerly waiting for this moment for a long time. He read the poem in a hushed murmur . . .

Walking along for a few steps
Gives the illusion of finding someone for life
The joy of finding him at the last turn
Was now dragging along
With the fear of losing him on the next
Like a shoe that pinches the foot on every step
A constant fear of—
Will he turn at this bend in the road?
If he stopped
So did my breath
Feet turning red and sore
Couldn't it just be a simple straight road?
Is there no end to
The desire for the next turn
That rose in the other
I wish I could drag this relationship
Back to the same turn in the road

Where we started this journey
And I would turn away
even before starting to walk with him
He would call after me
Call me Grief
But Grief listens to nobody . . .

Dushyant read the poem twice and when he raised his head to look at him, Rohit couldn't see any flower petals on his lips. His lips were wet, and sunflowers were peeking out of his eyes. Dushyant came near Rohit and that afternoon near the fort, by the riverside, under the peepal tree, they made love. They belonged to each other more than they could have ever belonged to anyone, and in between their racing breaths, they told one another, 'How beautiful this is,' but it meant something different for each of them.

26

It was raining heavily. I was making coffee and butter toast. Antima was listening to her favourite songs. It was like I had travelled back in time. Years ago, the same songs had played in the background when I had been making breakfast for Antima, and it had been raining as well. At the time, we were about to break up, and long silences punctuated our conversations.

'You need some help,' said Antima as she came into the kitchen.

'No, it's almost done.'

There's such freedom in this comfort. It takes knowing someone very well to find a home in them where you can be yourself. Antima and I had found that place inside each other.

'Why did you ask me to wear a saree? And what is this thread about?'

We went out and sat on the balcony. Antima was eating her breakfast when she asked me the question. I saw that a small bird had flown over and perched behind her. I was reminded of Dushyant's poem.

'I was stuck at some point in the story and needed some inspiration. I can't tell you about the green thread because the story hasn't reached that point yet.'

'Yes, but you can tell me at least.'

'That would be unfaithful to the story, I can't do that.'

'You can't tell me because you don't know either.'

'Yes, I truly don't know what's going on with the story.'

'Have you always been this anxious?'

'How's the toast?'

Antima smiled at my question. I received a text from Pawan. It was a reply to my last text: *Are you familiar with that lizard?*

I laughed at his reply.

'What?' Antima asked.

'Arey, that friend of mine. That guy who has become a friend. It's his text.'

'So, you're meeting him then? Be careful, who knows how many other people he is meeting.'

Antima was done with her toast. The rain had stopped. Birds were flying in the sky again. A deep quiet settled inside me in the evening. Sometimes I want to tell everyone everything about it, but what can you tell? I was already accused of being complicated. But I couldn't keep quiet.

'I'm riddled with guilt,' I said.

'What sort of guilt?' Antima was used to hearing me talk like this. She didn't pay much attention to it.

'Should I tell Pawan that I'm writing about him?'

'The guy who just texted you?'

'Yes, what should I do?'

'You can't do that.'

'What? Should I not tell him?'

'No, you can't put everyone who comes into your life into one of your stories. Who gave you the right to do that?'

'I'm changing the names, what else should I do?'

'If you change a word in some song and sing it yourself, does it become your original creation?'

'Those are two different things.'

'Yes, I think this is far worse.'

'So, what do you expect from a writer? Where should I draw inspiration from?'

'You write fiction, use your imagination.'

'But imagination too needs a foundation in reality. Where do I get that?'

'I don't know, but you can't just use someone else's life in your writing like this. That person will turn into a deaf-mute puppet in your hands. He'll say what you want him to; go where you want him to. It's a crime.'

Antima was upset. I knew where this debate would end up. I wanted it to stop, so I kept quiet. The rain had let up and the air was humid. I was sweating and it made me uncomfortable. I finished my coffee and sweat started to drip off my face.

'You're sweating a lot. Are you okay?' Antima asked.

'I'm fine!' Antima still looked as beautiful as she did when she arrived, as beautiful as I've ever known her to be. The way she was when I met her in Delhi for the first time.

'Why am I not sweating?' Antima said. I was caught by surprise.

'You're sweating.'

A drop of sweat rolled down her forehead all the way to her neck and disappeared. That was my mistake. Antima stood up with rage. I hung my head in defeat. When you dream, a feeling of discomfort rises in you which makes you question why things are happening the way they are. That's the moment you realize that you're dreaming, that none of it is real. So, you try to play with that discomfort and that's your flaw. The people who were a part of your dream so far, now resist being a part of it. All of them revolt and you have to open your eyes. I looked up at Antima. She was indignant. I shouldn't have asked her to wear a saree. I shouldn't have talked to her about Pawan. It wasn't him I was guilty about. I was guilty about her. I wanted her permission and she had finally realized it. Asking your characters for consent is the same as asking the people in your dreams for it. Your characters can smell your lies and your dream is shattered.

'Where am I right now?' Antima asked.

It would have been dangerous to answer so I stayed silent.

'Am I in Delhi?'

I still didn't say anything.

'Was all this a lie?'

She came closer.

'None of it is false. I'm living every bit of it with full conviction.'

'I asked you to never write about me.'

Antima slumped down in the chair in front of me. Why did it feel like I was using everybody, and I didn't care about anyone? I jumped into the dark well of my story with all my characters. I experienced their pain, and their laughter, more than I experienced my own. I couldn't bear to see Antima like this. I couldn't sit silently and avoid her questions.

'Do you remember the Vienna airport?' I said. 'I was in a queue for my flight, and you were standing nearby trying to contain your sobs. I couldn't bear you standing there helplessly. You gave me a forced smile, waved and went to the waiting room, so I ran after you, without any care about my flight, just to kiss you. Remember, I came to gather you, all your grief, your teary eyes, all the journeys I had taken with you . . . I just wanted to kiss you and take everything away, just to bring back that childish smile on your face. I've never written about it, ever.'

'But you just did.'

'If I don't, I'll never be able to get rid of you. You'll keep popping up in my writing with different names. If I don't write this now, then you'll keep haunting everything else I write. I'll have to end it by writing it.'

'Why are you so complicated?'

'Every way I can untangle my life, starts and ends with you.'

'You're not complicated, you're just plain selfish. You're only honest to your writing, and that's a tragedy.'

I wanted to apologize, but it would have been pointless. I knew she would never forgive me. She left without my permission.

How much of our normal life do we spend inside our heads, and how much of it outside, in the real world? Isn't it treacherous to our real lives? Imagination works inside all of us in the same way. My father always keeps a photograph of me and my mother in front of him, in which both of us are smiling. Every time we argued, he would end up saying that he couldn't talk to me anymore and that his real son was inside that picture. I would feel bad upon hearing that. Why couldn't he accept me completely? But now I know that nobody accepts anybody completely. Everyone uses half-truths and half-fiction; only then is it possible to maintain a constant connection with anyone. So, if I want to write the part of someone that's in my imagination, how is that selfish? I'm writing the part I know. I also wanted to get permission from that person, but I've observed that that is always dangerous. Can we ever ask the people we dream about if they have a problem with being a part of our dreams?

The lockdown had an absurd effect on me, everything echoed inside me for a long time, even if it was an argument I had with my own characters. I knew that I was writing a story that I was supposed to send to my editor as soon as I could. Other than that, the boundaries between reality and imagination were constantly blurring.

I had decided that whatever I wrote after this story would be about a stranger. Like the old man I saw on my walk every day, sitting on a bench in the park. I had only ever seen his back. He stared at the banyan tree in front of the bench for hours. I would write his story and this time there would be no issues regarding permissions: I didn't know him and he didn't know me.

I picked up my phone and texted Antima.

Please forgive me.

For what? Are you okay? What happened? she replied sometime later.

I'm good . . . it's nothing.

Idiot.

I could hear that 'idiot' written in her text. I stood for a long time on my balcony with my coffee, smiling like an idiot.

27

What time was it? What day was it? I had spent so many days lying around the house, I had no curiosity left to enquire about such details. All news was stale the minute it dropped. No headlines and no news stayed entertaining for people for more than a day. People sitting at home needed some sort of entertainment, as they too were unable to grasp the head or the tail of things these days. Every argument ended up erupting into a war on social media. China has entered Ladakh, Nepal had its own issues, and we and Pakistan were forever stuck in a never-ending tussle. Many of my friends had moved away, whereas some had decided to wait this out for a few more months. Everyone was of the opinion that all would be back to normal in a few days. The only helpful thing in all this was the knowledge that this virus was not that deadly. Whenever there was news of somebody's death, we had the same conversations again and again, but no, the virus wasn't that deadly. There was longing in everyone's eyes and the weariness of the wait as well. Every time the death toll increased, so did the number of people on the roads. The fear of the past few months had given rise to a monotony in people, and they were now stepping out of their homes to kill it. Everyone had gotten rid of their fear by wearing masks. The vegetable sellers, the grocers and the milkmen all shrugged off any discussion of the virus. Everyone was worried about making a living. For the first time, the future didn't hold that much importance; everyone was worried about their present. They were worried about today, now. They were worried about selling their wares before they spoiled.

When everything was fine, all the politicians and rich people assured us that the societal structure where everyone was constantly working and only a select few were growing richer and richer, was the best form of society there could be. And, if anybody ever tried to change anything, it would all come crashing down. But they were all lying. Now we know that a society can function in myriad ways. We can run the world all different ways. Marx wasn't wrong, nor were all the other people who could see that this way of running the world wasn't right. We can have a number of other systems, in which the power won't be controlled by a select few but can be divided from the very bottom to the very top.

I could tell that Salim was getting progressively worried. I told him that I could come there but he thought I was too busy in Mumbai. Like, even in this situation, he thought I was running from meeting to meeting. I tried to explain to him that I could come, but he had more authority in all these decisions. He told me he was going to start living with my father in a few days. He wouldn't go back to his house. My father was happy when he heard I might visit but he was also worried about all the arguments that might break out between us at any moment. And if I was buzzing around him day and night, it would only worsen the situation. These days, I called my father one day and Salim the next, and listened to both of them while I cooked, did the dishes and tidied the house. My father said the virus had started to spread in Kashmir, but it wouldn't have much effect there. *The air and the water here contain the blood of many people, so the virus won't be able to stay.* I had nothing to say when he said such things. Then he asked me with a child-like curiosity what kind of dreams I was having these days. As a writer, I could make up any dream one could conceive, or one my father would have liked to hear about, but I didn't want to do that to him. I thought about asking him for permission, now that I was writing him into my story, but I didn't.

A text came from Aru: *If I name you Komal, will all the touches be soft like you?*

I replied with a *very beautiful* and decided to meet Pawan.

I had received an email from my editor.

You should finish your story soon. People want to read it now. It's the perfect time for short stories; just send whatever you've written so far . . . I'll edit it as you go.

I attached the part of the story that I had in the email, but before sending it over, I decided I wasn't the one writing it. Verma Madam's point of view was not the same as mine. Whatever she could see, from her window into the story—clouds, river, trees— everything was an extension of Dushyant's body. Whenever I tried to step inside the forest that was Dushyant, my feet would give way. All I could do was wait. I sometimes wondered, what if Dushyant could tell this story from his side, his own little window, what could he have seen? I was trying to hide the real story behind a love story. But Verma Madam had said everything that I tried to hide out loud. And if Dushyant had written this, then he would have lived, or more likely tolerated every word of it, as he had tolerated me. I pressed *send,* and with that also bid farewell to all my thoughts.

I was going to see Pawan, and I thought of asking Aru what she was doing at the moment. While crossing the park, I saw the same bench again and the same old man sitting on it. A character for my next story . . . Could I sit down by his side and relax for a bit? Could I share my worries about my present story with the character of my next? No, I didn't want to pollute my next story with this one. I pulled out my phone and texted Aru, asking if I could listen to the whole poem. I saw Pawan walking towards me; he had a plastic bag wrapped around his head.

'Why are you wearing this bag?'

'It can rain any time and I want to save my hair.'

'Why?'

'No bigger sorrow than losing one's hair.'

Everything Pawan said had a bleak tone to it. We started walking. We had walked a little when he said, 'Today we'll turn right and walk around the back.'

'Why?'

'We should keep our eyes and our body alert, or they'll get used to the rut of the routine and grow lazy. There should always be little shocks to keep everything alert; that way our senses are always ready to face any danger.'

'What danger?'

'This virus. Do you know that India is at number three? And believe me, this virus is affecting those whose bodies are in a state of tranquillity, stuck in the same routine.'

We started walking around the back. The roads were muddy and where Pawan was walking, the surface was broken as well. I wanted to ask Pawan to turn back. I wanted to walk in peace, but here we had to watch out for the mud. I was getting irritated now. But before I could say anything, he asked me, 'Have you killed the lizard yet?'

'No.'

'Why?'

'Arey, how can I kill it?'

'Just pick up a *chappal* and do it. Did you not learn anything from my experience?'

Pawan was not happy with this; it was a big issue for him.

'I'm fine with the lizard.' I said, trying to defuse the situation.

'At first, I also felt that way, but the thing is, you're alone now, you need companionship. Do you understand me?'

'No, I don't think I do.'

'The lizard knows that you live alone. These days it keeps away from homes with families. They're attracted to lonely, single people, who are hungry for companionship.'

'I'm not hungry,' I said, trying to refute his allegation.

'You, my friend, are gravely mistaken.'

'No, it's the truth.'

'Then tell me this . . . how did we end up becoming such good friends? Would you have texted and asked to spend time with me if not for this lockdown?'

I had nothing to say to this. Pawan was one of those people whose thought process worked backwards. You couldn't argue with them, there was no winning with them. If I were to enjoy my evening walk, I'd have to agree with everything he said. I just wanted to go back to the same route we used to take. This one was muddy and dark.

'Yes, you're right.'

'You'll notice that when you're ruined from the inside, you'll find the lizard everywhere. It will suddenly appear in those corners of your home where you cry. Then you won't wonder where it came from. You'll like having any living being near you. But the companionship will be short-lived. The minute you start to feel better, it will run away. So, the next time, when you're sad, you'll look for the lizard again, and that will mean that the lizard has won and that is its real mission.'

'What mission is that?' By then I completely believed him.

'The mission is for you to accept them. Accept that they're an important part of your home. And then you'll find yourself thinking along the lines that the world belongs to everyone. That all of us have an equal right over this world. All this is done by lizards. They ask for their right, their part, in return for taking your loneliness away. And that day is not far when in a weak moment you'll find yourself talking to them. No one shows such affection to spiders, cockroaches, ants or mosquitoes. You can easily kill them and experience no guilt. But lizards trick you with their tinny noises and their skill at reading the human mind.'

'Have you ever talked to a lizard?' I asked.

Pawan went silent. I removed my mask and took some deep breaths. At times, you feel suffocated after wearing the mask for a long time. But here I took my mask off, so that he would take off his as well, and I would be able to see his face. People's faces are different in silence. His eyes betrayed no emotion, there was a terrifying calm in them instead. He pulled his mask down, took some breaths and put it back up. I could only get a glimpse of his silent face. Should I tell him that I was writing about him in my story? I had a strong urge to come clean with it when it started raining. We both ran and took shelter under a shed outside the cobbler's shop. The shop was closed.

'I used to talk to Asha and Manohar,' Pawan said after some time.

'Who are they?'

'The two lizards I killed first.'

Whenever it rained heavily, I remembered the day my mother died. Silent faces of mourners with hundreds of eyes, searching for a deep sadness within me. There's a weird pull in other people's pain . . . it disturbs us if we can't find that pain in their eyes at the right time. A son having a normal conversation like any other day makes us uncomfortable. I was reminded of Camus' book *The Outsider*. I wanted to read the Borges poem that I kept inside it; I wanted to read it now. Pawan took his mask off, and I could see there were tears in his eyes. I realized that I was no different from those relatives of mine who wanted to see me cry. I looked at the people on the road who were running hunched up due to the rain as if doing that would save them from the water. I received a text from Aru: *Whenever you want to . . .*

I smiled at the message.

'Is it Aru?' Pawan asked.

'Yeah,' I said and put my phone back in my pocket.

'What is she saying?' Pawan sounded suspicious. He might have seen the text.

'I haven't seen her in a long time so . . .' I tried to skirt past it.

'Is she asking you to come over?'

'Yes, I'll go see her.'

'Then let's go together.'

'Right now?'

'Yes, she's asking you to come, right? Do one thing, tell her that you're coming. She'll be surprised when she sees me.'

If it hadn't been raining, I would have just gone home. But I was stuck under this shed with Pawan.

'No, it's fine. I'll see her later. I have some work.'

'You're the worst liar, man! Now take that phone out and text her that you're coming over.'

The rain was slowing down. Pawan was so excited about his idea that he didn't budge even after I objected multiple times. I texted Aru that I was coming over. Aru sent me a lot of heart emojis that Pawan didn't see. We started walking towards her house. Pawan had a spring in his step; he looked like he was about to run, and maybe he even did a little. The inability to refuse him had made something burst inside me. It made me angry at Pawan. I had no idea what would happen at her house. What would she think of me bringing Pawan along? Pawan pressed the button for the lift, and it started to descend towards us.

'I want to tell you something,' I said to Pawan.

'Yeah, say.'

'I'm writing about you.'

'What do you mean?'

'I mean you're a part of the story I'm writing. I thought it was better to tell you.'

'Are you done writing, or will you start now?'

'I'm writing . . . right this moment, I'm writing about you.'

Pawan removed his mask. He was staring at me like a bird who had spotted itself in a mirror. The lift had arrived. I was about to enter the lift when he stopped me.

'Am I a villain in your story?' he asked me.

'It's not that kind of a story; there's no hero or villain.'

We entered the lift.

'Are there lizards in your story?' he asked after a minute.

'Yes.'

'Do you take permission from everyone you write into your stories?'

'It's fiction; there's no need to ask for permission.'

'So what is this?'

'I just thought I should ask.'

'Ask me if you can write anything about me?'

'It's not anything, it's a story.'

'But it's fictional, right? So you have the liberty to write anything using my name?'

'I can change your name if you want.'

'And what about the lizard? Will you change it to a cockroach?'

We had reached the sixth floor. Pawan rang the bell. Aru opened the door with a smile, but it vanished as soon she saw Pawan.

'Surprise!' shouted Pawan.

Aru didn't take long to bring back the smile. I couldn't look her in the eye. I saw she had decorated the place with tiny, beautiful diyas. She was wearing a black frock-like dress. Two glasses of wine were placed on the balcony, and one could hear light music as well.

'I was telling Rohit that I don't want to come but he insisted on surprising you,' said Pawan. I looked at him with surprise. When Aru went to get a glass for Pawan, he came to me and whispered in my ear, 'If you can write lies, I can tell them too.'

I was kicking myself. Just then, Salim messaged me: *It's Father's Day today. He's waiting for your call.* I felt a pang inside me. I looked up at the sky. The dark clouds had subsided, and I could see stars.

'Cheers!' we said, clinking our glasses together.

'You're looking very beautiful,' Pawan said to Aru.

'I was bored of wearing everyday clothes in lockdown, so I wanted to dress up today.'

She said this looking at me. She didn't have any right to complain to me, but she could still show that she was mad at me. But I wasn't really there; I was thinking of my father. Pawan was talking about the benefits of wearing a plastic bag on one's head and we were listening to him. How many times had I called my father on Father's Day? Earlier, Ma used to remind me. I felt like a part of me hung from the old hook at home, watching my father sitting near the phone. If I didn't call him now, he would've gone to sleep by the time I did, and it would be more painful for me if he stayed up waiting for the call. I couldn't be a part of Aru and Pawan's conversation for long. I called my father and walked to the other corner of the roof.

'Happy Father's Day, Daddy,' I said when he picked up the call.

'Oh, you remembered? I thought you must be busy, so I didn't want to disturb you by calling. What is this Father's Day anyway? Any day you call is Father's Day for me.'

We can do so little for our parents. This thought was the root of a painful twinge of irritation that rose from deep within my body, somewhere between my belly and my back. You keep scratching, but the twinge doesn't go away, like a sneeze stuck halfway. You never feel fully satisfied by the fact that you loved them completely. It always troubles you that you couldn't ever fully experience the time you have with them.

'I fell asleep in the afternoon and dreamt about Kashmir. This is the first time I've dreamt about Kashmir in the daytime,' I said.

'Was I in the dream?

'Yes.'

'And your mother?'

'She was there too.'

We always want to speak truthfully and love truthfully. But at some point, the truth turns so monotonous you can't squeeze any more love out of it. If I'd truthfully said that I'd forgotten about today, this moment would have hurt him so much it would have been impossible to heal the wound.

'A dream in the daytime is good.' My father was excited.

'Yes, I saw snow in the dream. In the soft light of the sun, snow shimmered all around me.'

I stayed silent for a minute. What more should I say? It was easy for me to venture into the lanes of Kashmir, to wander in my mind wherever I wanted. Pawan was talking to Aru in another corner of the terrace, whereas her focus was on me. Suddenly the door to Aru's bedroom opened and I saw a deer on her bed. I thought it would walk towards me, but it just stayed there, as if waiting for me to approach. I saw that the deer had white eyes, and when I looked closely, I saw snow in them. And in that snow, I saw a man in a blue winter coat walking back to his home.

'Then?' my father said from the other end.

'You had on your blue winter coat, and you had just walked back home. Ma brought out tea and Krackjack biscuits for the three of us. We made space in the snow and sat down to have tea. I sat in your lap and your beard pricked me. You were rubbing my shoulders with your warm hands because I was shivering from the cold.'

'Yes, you were really cold on snowy days.'

In the deer's eyes, I saw my father sitting inside his house in the village. His eyes were stuffed with cotton. From afar it gave the false impression of snow. He was shivering, his old phone stuck to his ear. He was trying to stand and touch the dream I was telling him about, but the phone had a small cord, and he fell again and again. I felt a chill run down my spine.

'We left the snow and came back to sit inside the room that had the bukhari, but the room wouldn't heat up because the glass in one window was shattered. All the heat was escaping from that broken window. I went and sat in that window and looked out at the smoke coming from the bukhari. The swirling smoke made it look like all of Kashmir was burning. You kept saying Kashmir is so beautiful, but people are burning it all just to get rid of the cold. You put out the bukhari and lit the kangri and hid me in your phiran. I burnt my hand on the kangri. That's when you gave me your blue winter coat for the first time. I put it on as I cried, but the happiness of wearing it made the pain go away. That night you listened to Rafi songs till late and we all slept together under a single quilt.'

My father needed a happy ending. I saw in the eyes of the deer that my father was looking for something in his almirah. He found some yellowed photographs of our old house. He was holding them tightly in his hands. After that, the deer's eyes turned deep brown, and I stopped talking.. My eyes welled up; one by one, all the lies, guilt and shame dripped down.

'And then I woke up. It felt so good to wake up, I can't even explain it to you.'

'Why are you crying?'

'No, why would I cry?'

'When everything is okay, you and I will go to Kashmir . . . we'll take Salim with us too.'

'Yes, sure. Happy Father's Day.'

'Give my love to Aru.'

'Yes.'

I took a deep breath and slid the phone back into my pocket. I walked towards Pawan and Aru. The deer still stood in Aru's bedroom waiting for me. I was shivering. My body was marked with red rashes from my time in Kashmir and they responded to the cold. I finished my wine in one go. Aru was saying something to me, but I couldn't hear her. These days wherever I set foot, it becomes hard to distinguish whether the earth under my feet is real or not. I shouldn't have told Pawan that I was writing him into my story, but it was pointless to talk to him now. Was Aru here?

'I want to talk to you about something,' I said to Aru.

'Yeah, tell me.'

'Not here, somewhere alone.'

'Pawan, we'll be back in two minutes.'

Pawan looked at me and lifted his wine glass with 'cheers'. I directed Aru towards her bedroom, 'What happened?' asked Aru.

There was no deer in the bedroom, I could see its footprints on the sheet though. I took her hand and pulled her towards me.

'What time is it? What day is it today? You're here, right?' I asked with a shudder.

Aru could see a certain madness in my eyes, I could see the recognition in her eyes. Her mouth opened a little. It was a if she knew what was going to happen next and everything seemed superficial to her. I wanted to leave that very moment. Aru placed her hands on my face and slowly started to touch me. I was looking at her as if it was she who had led me to the bedroom and not the other way around. She closed my eyes. I was going to kiss her, but she stopped me. She was unbuttoning my shirt. By then I had surrendered to her. She slowly removed my clothes and laid me down on her bed. I realized that I was part of a play that Aru was writing. I didn't open my eyes because one mistake could turn me into a spectator. Soon she came near me. I could feel her breath on different parts of my body. She was hovering all over it, maybe she was looking for a space for herself in me. The first touch was on my shoulder, and I had goosebumps. Soon I realized that she wasn't wearing any clothes either. I wanted to see her naked at that very moment, but I also didn't want to stop being a part of this play, so I kept my eyes closed. I opened my eyes when I entered Aru. She was on top of me, and her hair fell on my face. It felt like I had opened a window on a rainy day and put my face out into the downpour. At this point in the play, I remembered that I had forgotten to shut

the door. As I turned my head to look, I thought I would find
the deer standing there. But it wasn't there, instead, Pawan
stood in the doorway, like a spectator. Was I writing Pawan
standing in the doorway? Was Aru even there? I gently pulled
Aru towards me by her hair and started to kiss her. I could
touch her. She was around me . . . it wasn't all imaginary. I
started thinking, have I witnessed this scene before? No, but
I had imagined that one day Verma Madam and Dushyant
would leave the door to their room open, and I'd witness
their bodies entwining like this. I turned her around and laid
her on her back. She looked at the door. Could she also see
Pawan standing there? I wanted her to look at the door before
I kissed her. Aru looked at me. I turned her face towards the
door again. I wanted Dushyant and Verma Madam to see me
when they were entwined with one another. Aru was looking
towards the door, and I felt like I was standing at the door.
I wanted to take revenge on myself, on my childhood. Then
I felt that it was not me who was standing at the door, but
Dushyant and I were in bed with Verma Madam. The mere
thought of it made me scream. Aru tried to cover my mouth.
She didn't want the voice to go outside. But I wasn't in control
anymore. Aru wanted to look at me, but I turned her face
towards the door every time she did. There was a madness
in imagining Dushyant standing in the doorway. Soon there
was an explosion and I felt as if it had just snowed inside
Aru's room. Everything was so white that it was blinding. I
couldn't see anything in that brilliant whiteness. I fell beside
Aru and realized that I needed to take some deep breaths,
or I'd choke. I started to gasp for air like a hungry child. I
closed my eyes. I had fallen out of the comfort of Kashmir's
soft snow and directly into deep water. I was swimming in

the river now. Far away, under the water, I could see a man collecting coins. When I swam near him, I saw that it was Dushyant, and he wasn't collecting coins but dead fish. I was happy to see Dushyant, but he couldn't see me. He was extremely busy with what he was doing. He was storing the dead fish in his mouth like we did with the coins we found in the river. Dushyant's mouth was so full that it was about to burst. I looked upwards, above the surface, where the deer stood on the riverbank and a stream of dead lizards poured from its eyes. I left Dushyant and started swimming towards the deer, but no matter how hard I tried, I couldn't break above the surface. I thrashed and thrashed, and suddenly found myself back in Aru's bed with a jolt. I could hear the shower coming from the bathroom. The snow had melted away from the room. Nobody stood at the door. Aru wasn't beside me. The fan wasn't turning, but I could feel a cool breeze on my face. The moment I heard the bathroom door opening, I closed my eyes.

28

I sometimes saw the old man walk slowly to the far-off bench outside the park. Every few minutes he would adjust his glasses and look at the bench as if to check if it was still there and wasn't just a figment of his imagination. He would then take a few more steps and stop to catch his breath again. When he was about to reach the bench, a thought must have occurred to him that he had not yet decided what he would do once he reached the bench. Whom would he call? Whom would he talk to? What a waste, to reach here after such an effort and still be unable to decide what it is that he wanted to do once he was there! I started spinning a story around the old man. His reaching the bench looked a lot like my writing to me. You proceed from one sentence to another, then stop for hours to catch your breath. You can see the end of the story, but you can't decide if it's there or not. And just when you're about to reach the end, you forget whom you want to read this story to once you are done with it. Why did you write it in the first place? Who was it that you hoped to meet at the end of the story, on the bench?

A writer has many fears. But his biggest fear is that one day he'll finish everything he has to write and be alone. A writer is never able to bear the loneliness he feels when he finishes something he's writing. To avoid this, he starts to imagine the next home long before he leaves the first. He just wants to save himself from that feeling of emptiness. If you read someone's writing carefully, then at the end of one story you'll easily find the signs pointing to their next. Writing is a trap. It's an addiction; once you get a taste, you never feel alive without it. I think it's the effect of this lockdown that I was unable to hide anything. I wrote about seeing the old man from my next story in this story. Can I tell this story that once I'm done with you, I'll go to the park bench to rest?

For the past few days, whenever I stepped out to buy something for the house, I saw so many people out and about that if I wasn't paying attention to the news, everything would have felt normal. People have assimilated the pandemic into their lifestyle, their clothes and their conduct. The conjecture about a possible cure has given people hope. Hope is like a piece of candy you can keep sucking on for days and even months. This virus will make its way through all of us. Maybe people had come to terms with this truth while enjoying their piece of candy. There were thousands of new cases every day. And the number was about to climb to lakhs. But the fear was going away.

I only stepped out of the house to run the important errands. In the end, I came back to my story. I wandered around words but couldn't write anything. The most dangerous thing is to fall for your own characters. I don't know what I'll do without them anymore. What strange violence to inflict on oneself, to build something from scratch and then watch it end in front of your eyes. These wounds hurt for a long time. Can't we write a single story till the end? Or maybe we're all writing a single story till the very end.

When I woke up in the morning, I saw I had a text waiting from my father. He had sent it at ten past three in the night. I opened the text. He had asked: *Does your mother visit you in your dreams?* There are some sentences which live with you. You can't shrug them off your body easily. The whole day I couldn't find an answer to his question. I always thought that my mother, my father and I were three corners of a triangle, where the line connecting me and my mother only belonged to the two of us, the same way the line connecting my parents was the part of the house where I wasn't allowed to enter. When my father asked such questions, he was seeking entry into that room of the house that had previously been inaccessible to him. These are the conversations that make people uncomfortable in relationships. Some houses are completely open to all of their residents but ours was not such a house. Our house stood on the foundation of the mutual strain between the sides of the triangle. It was evening when I wrote back: *Sometimes in beautiful dreams I see her smiling face.* I had said this to make my father happy. That night at Aru's house, I had dug a hole in the wall of truth by lying about that dream of Kashmir. Now lies have entered our conversation. It's the first lie that hurts. Once that one has made it through, it becomes an everyday occurrence, and the lies start to smell like the truth itself, and we aren't too bothered anymore. It's like Pawan killing that first lizard. It's the first death that hurts.

I couldn't ignore the emails from my editor any longer. If I started writing replies, I would have to write a lot. I decided it was better to call.

'Namaste,' he said when he picked up the call.

'Namaste, sorry I couldn't reply to your emails. I thought I'd simply call you.'

'Yes, I like this story, and it's important to add it to the collection, but you must make haste. Everything is on pause because of this one story.'

He was busy, I thought. I could hear some people talking around him.

'Have you started going to the office? I mean has work there resumed?' I was trying to avoid discussing the story.

'Yes, we had to start someday. So tell me, how far has the story progressed?'

'Yes, it'll be done really soon. I'll only send the rest to you when it's all done. That's why it's taking a bit of time.'

'Yes, please hurry. Whatever part of the story you have sent so far has already been edited.'

I promised to send him the story soon and hung up. I could see the end and I had started walking towards it as well. When my mother used to read my poems, she would always ask me why I didn't write simply. What she meant was why didn't I write happy, optimistic poems, ones which rhymed and sounded like proper poems? Even today if I think about writing a simple poem with a rhyme scheme, Dushyant's angry face comes to me. But with this story, I had tried really hard to stay on this side of the river. Just write a simple story about a few innocent moments of guileless childhood. However, the characters' intervention in the writing process ruined everything. We shouldn't converse with our characters outside the story. They can sense our weaknesses and fears. Like if the horse you're riding senses your fear, it'll throw you off and then you'll be dragged behind the horse. I was being dragged too.

29

I put on my shoes and went out for a walk. I looked up at the sky: a lone eagle was soaring near the horizon. The sky around it was red. I took some more steps and looked up to see that the sky had changed. There were new patterns in the red now. Nature constantly creates new spectacles and then changes them into something else. That's why I find nature closer to theatre. Anything that's happening a certain way at a given time won't happen again the same way. I was thinking about all the plays I had seen as I passed by the park. I saw the old man sitting on the bench outside the park. Maybe he was waiting for this story to end as well. I didn't want to start his story, but I had a desire to see his face once. I kept walking. I had to stay in the present story. I reached the road where I used to walk with Pawan. I went to the end of the road to wait for him. In the sky, the eagle was almost invisible among a murder of crows. Many old people were walking here with masks on their faces. Sometimes, young people who were running and cycling passed these old people. The virus had struck the elderly with immense fear. Their strides had shrunk, and life had seeped out of them.

'Were you waiting for me?' Pawan's voice came from behind.

I turned around and saw that Pawan wasn't wearing a mask. He started walking and I accompanied him.

'You aren't wearing a mask?' I asked.

'You should remove yours too. This virus will get to everyone, there's no escaping it. What good will it do to inhale our own carbon dioxide?'

I pulled my mask down. For a long time, we kept walking in silence. I tried to break the silence.

'Are you planning to go back to your village now that travelling is allowed?'

'Do you even know how the virus has spread? In terms of case numbers, we're quickly rising to number two worldwide from number three.' He interrupted my train of thought. We crossed the park and I looked at the old man again. This time I tried but still couldn't see his face. We reached the road on the other side; you could see the open sky from there.

'Do you know Mumbai has a special quality?' Pawan said, 'You go to any city in the country and ask someone how far something is and the reply you'll get would be that the place is so and so kilometres away. But if you asked the same question in Mumbai, you'd be told that this or that place was such and such minutes away. Here people measure distance with time and not with kilometres. That's how important time is for this city. That's why, now that people suddenly have too much of it on their hands, they don't know what to do with it. And that's the reason for the weird reactions we're seeing. People are behaving out of character.'

I couldn't understand what he was talking about or whom. I nodded my assent to whatever he said and kept walking alongside him. I just wanted to spend enough time with him to let go of all the pain from that night. We kept going round and round on the back road for a while. Then at one turn, he stopped.

'I should go now. There's something important I need to do.'

I didn't say anything in response. As he left, he said, 'If you ever write about that night, please remove me from the scene. I don't want to see myself there.' Then he left. I started walking back to my house. I had already written everything. There had been incidents in the past where I didn't want to be a witness, but I was there regardless. I couldn't go into the past and omit my presence. Would Pawan ever forgive me? Was I eligible to ask for forgiveness from any of my characters? When I looked at the sky, I could see the stars. The darkness of the clouds in the moonlight and stars provided a dramatic setting to the whole thing. That's when Salim texted me. He had sent a photo, and the caption was: *Father has asked me to send it to you.* I saw that it was my birth certificate, which had yellowed with time. This was the first time I had seen this. Saint Joseph Hospital, Srinagar. And under it was my name, my date of birth and the time of birth was ten past three. I laughed. Every ripple in our life is intrinsically connected to the umbilical cord. The story starts the minute we're born. It's like a riddle, the solution to which we learn throughout our lives, in instalments.

I was crossing by the park. I looked over at the bench, which was now engulfed in darkness, and I saw that the old man was still sitting there. I stopped. I couldn't suppress the

desire to look at his face at that moment. When I reached
the bench, I was surprised to see that it was a woman. From
the back, she looked like an old man due to her white kurta
pyjama. When she turned towards me, she could see the
surprise on my face.

'I'm alive,' she said.

'No, sorry, I thought . . . let it be.'

'If I don't move for a long time, it seems like I'm dead.
That's why I think it's better to say it upfront.'

'That's not what I thought.'

She tried to get up but even after two attempts she
couldn't. When I tried to help, she raised her hand to stop
me. Her breathing was sharp.

'It'll take me a while to get up. You can go, I can leave
by myself,' she said, the words flying out of her mouth like
half-dead birds.

'Can I sit here for a minute? Not to help you, not for you,
but because I need to sit.'

She motioned for me to sit. I sat down beside her.
I would've left, but I was sad about the fact that we're so
polluted from the inside. Our male-dominated society has
such an effect on us that even after seeing her so many times
from behind . . . I couldn't imagine her as a woman. At first
sight, we only see men as our main characters. I sat beside her,
my head hanging in shame. There was a tall peepal tree in
front of me and a huge banyan tree stood behind it, its roots
spreading all over the walls around it. Sitting here might be a
calming experience in the day, but in the dark, the air flowing
through the leaves resulted in eerie music, which made the
entire place feel deserted. I saw that she picked up a dry leaf,
which floated toward her with the wind, and put it in her lap.

Her hands and fingers were extremely soft. She caressed the leaf in her lap as though it had been lying wounded on the road for days.

'My granddaughter came to me one day and asked what I would change if I could change anything from my youth. Young people ask that a lot. I said I wouldn't change anything, I'm happy with the life I've lived so far. She was happy with my answer, but the question got stuck in my head. What would I have changed?'

I felt as if she was talking to the leaf. My being there was a mere coincidence. She looked at me after some time, like I was the one who had asked her the question. This was the first time I was looking at her face this closely. I felt as if someone had affixed a young pair of eyes there. They were filled with a strange playfulness that refused to lose its shine even in the dark.

'What would you change?' I asked.

'Everything, everything, like a maniac. I can say that to you. When we say such things to our families, everything changes its meaning.'

I saw a lizard climb up the leg of the bench and rest near her knee. She let go of the leaf and placed a finger near the lizard. The lizard touched her finger with its mouth once or twice, then placed a foot on her finger, and then stopped for a while, as though waiting for the right time. Then suddenly it jumped into her hand. She placed the lizard on the leaf and stared at it. This world would have ended long ago if, amid all the cruelties that befall us, there had not also been pure and innocent love.

'She's been wandering around for many days now, and since a few days ago she started to come and sit by me. Animals take a lot of time to trust human beings.'

She said this while caressing the lizard's neck with her fingers. I felt that there was a melody in all this, the same as the one I experienced when I wrote. A minute dance was happening inside me with the joy of finding my next story. I didn't notice when she put the leaf and the lizard back on the ground, took my hand to get up and we started walking back to our homes. It all happened very quickly. It turned out that she lived near my house. I walked her to her building's lift. She said, 'Don't accompany me further or my family will think that there's something going on between us.'

I laughed at this. As the doors of the lift closed, I told her my name: 'I'm Rohit by the way.' She smiled as if she already knew.

I wanted to ask hers but couldn't gather the courage. She was going upwards with the lift, and I was watching her perplexed.

I wasn't writing any of this. I was existing near my writing. For the first time, I was facing a world that was as tangled up as the wet kite string on the terrace of my childhood home. Simplicity is only attainable by those animals who are constantly registering their presence in our world. I was pacing in front of my computer when I felt that my feet weren't touching the ground; they were floating an inch and a half above the floor. I was holding my second glass of wine and half a cigarette. I wanted to dive deep after many days. After many days I wished to collect the coins of my story and hold them in my mouth. I sat in front of my computer and looked at the blank part of the story with a smile. I placed my hands on the keyboard and wrote a word: dargah. I kept staring at it.

'We live only a quarter of our life.' Verma Madam was beside me. I could experience her in all her beauty.

'I knew you must be around.' I didn't take my hands away from the keys.

'What happened at the dargah?' she whispered in my ear.

'I thought you knew.'

'A quarter of our life consists of many such portions that are patched up with imagination. This is one such portion for me. Whenever I was alone on my terrace having tea, and you wouldn't show up, I would imagine that you were writing your own poems and that justified me drinking tea on my own. But then you would come back and tell me that you had gone to the bazaar instead. Then I had to switch the poetry writing-Rohit of my imagination with the market going-Rohit. Only then would I feel that I was completely living every portion of my life. In reality, we get to see, taste and touch so little. Our imagination is what fills up the gaps in our experiences, or else a part of our life would seem meaningless to us.'

'The biggest part of my imagination were the times when you and Dushyant would be in your room, and I would walk around on the terrace alone.'

'No, you stood on the other side of the closed door, listening to our whispers and sounds.'

I pulled my hands away from the keyboard and picked up the glass of wine.

'What should I write?' I didn't want to ask this.

'Write what you don't want to,' Verma Madam replied.

'Can't we change the ending?' I pleaded.

'Why step into lanes that are closed?'

'I know why you're here!'

'Because I want to know the ending as well, but the one that actually happened and not the one made of a writer's artifice.'

'Why was there a painting of a deer on your wall?'

'I never had any painting of a deer on my wall.'

How neatly we arrange our fears in our imagination. We feel that if we let our fears be a part of any other stories, they'd lose their intensity. But I wish stories were like us human beings and believed all our lies. When all our lives we have experienced various fears at different points, how could stories rid us of those fears? I placed a hand on Verma Madam's wrist and touched the green thread.

30

Dushyant was passing between Verma Madam and Rohit, like soft sunlight gently caressing their bodies on a beautiful cool day. The day belonged to both of them but because it was passing, both wanted to lay claim to it. Rohit was trying to calculate, something he was very bad at, but he came to the conclusion that if the nights belonged to Verma Madam, then Dushyant's days should be spent with him. But he couldn't say any of this in front of them. Even spending the day with Dushyant was proving difficult for Rohit. The time of the day when they went to the river, which only belonged to Dushyant and him, was now being taken over by Verma Madam as she too tagged along with them, her thesis work in tow. It all came to a head when he had to spend some evenings strolling on his terrace alone with both of them absent. The time when Dushyant would have to leave was fast approaching. When Verma Madam was there, Rohit couldn't find any flower

petals on Dushyant's lips. He tried communicating
with Dushyant via signals while trying not to be seen
by Verma Madam. But Dushyant wouldn't look at him
long enough to be able to interpret the signals.

Rohit wanted to steal some time away, in which
he and Dushyant would be together in the quiet.
Harsh sun would fall on their naked bodies and when
it suddenly rained, there would be water everywhere,
both outside the river and within it and in that water, he
would whisper some words he had written to Dushyant
and see flowers bloom on his lips.

Dushyant was going to leave the next day. The
school vacations were ending as well. Rohit was trying
to keep his composure. It was afternoon. Verma
Madam sat on the riverbank, watching both of them
dive deep into the water. Whenever Dushyant found
any coins, he would show them to Verma Madam like a
child and she clapped for him. For the first time, Rohit
found a one-rupee coin in the river, behind a rock. Still
underwater, he showed it to Dushyant, who took it
from him and came up to show it to Verma Madam,
as if he was the one who had found it. Rohit started
fighting with Dushyant.

'I found it . . . but he took it from me.'

'He's lying,' Dushyant said and laughed.

The three of them couldn't stop laughing. Rohit
climbed on top of Dushyant to take his coin back.
Dushyant started to go underwater because of Rohit's
weight. He tried to come up to breathe but Rohit kept
pushing him, 'Return my coin or I won't let you go.'
After a while when Dushyant couldn't bear it anymore,

he released the coin. Both of them were panting when they somehow reached Verma Madam and lay down by her side. Dushyant had turned red and was breathing hard. Verma Madam touched Dushyant's head and asked him, 'Are you okay?'

Dushyant kissed Verma Madam's hand and looked at her with a smile. Rohit had never seen Dushyant look this beautiful. The way he was looking at Verma Madam made something explode inside him. The explosion was full of shards of jealousy which were sharp and pricked him inside.

'Can we go to the other side of the river to steal watermelons?' Rohit asked to break the spell between them.

'No, let's go back home . . .' Verma Madam started gathering her books.

'The watermelons from our village are famous all over the country. If you don't steal them, can you even enjoy their taste?'

'The river is extremely wide. It seems difficult to me.'

'I've been across many times, it's very easy,' Rohit lied.

'I can't do it.' Dushyant lay down on his back.

'Okay, then I'll go on my own. You two keep looking at each other.' Rohit couldn't stop himself and the jealousy and anger that was inside him had erupted for the first time. He stood up and jumped into the river. Rohit was swimming and cursing himself for saying all that. He was disgusted by the jealousy he felt and anger propelled him to move his hands with such ferocity that he didn't know where he was headed and why. He would thrash his limbs and take deep breaths, then dive under the water and curse himself. In all this, he suddenly ran into something and swallowed some water. He stopped to cough and found himself in the middle of the river. He had never swum this far out. The minute he stopped, he felt an unbearable pain in his body and found it difficult to breathe. When he looked back, he saw that Dushyant was slowly swimming towards him. Verma Madam stood worried at the bank. The moment he saw Dushyant, all his exhaustion vanished. Slowly, Dushyant reached him. When Rohit looked at Dushyant's face, he saw it was ruddy and his eyes were full of fear.

'We'll go slowly, stopping at intervals. Half is already done, only half the distance is left.'

Dushyant nodded his assent and they started to slowly move towards the other bank. Rohit would stop for Dushyant now and then, letting him hold onto his shoulders to rest and catch a breath.

'We're almost there . . . just a few more strokes and we'll reach the sandy part.'

On the far side of the river, one encountered a sandy bank quite early. Soon Rohit felt sand under his feet. He stood on the sand bed to show Dushyant that they had reached. But it took Dushyant a long time to cover the small distance. The moment his feet touched the sand, he lost control and fell on Rohit. Rohit dragged him out onto the bank. Both of them lay on the warm sand. Once he caught his breath, Dushyant started to jump up and down to express his joy to Verma Madam who was on the other side. Rohit too waved at her.

'Let's go, I want to show you something,' Rohit said.

'No, let's go back, she must be worried,' Dushyant said, trying to brush the sand off of his body.

'We can't go now. Our bodies are tired and if we swim now, the exhaustion will come rushing back. Come, there's a beautiful jungle in the back.'

A dense forest stood on that side of the river. Dushyant tried to signal to Verma Madam that they'd be back soon, but she was looking as tiny as a dot now. He didn't know if she could even see him or not.

Rohit entered the forest. Dushyant was walking behind him. Sunlight filtered through the canopy of trees and fell on the round rocks on the ground. The breeze was cool here. Dushyant felt like he had suddenly dropped into a hill station after being in extreme heat. He looked around at the immense beauty of the forest when suddenly his feet made contact with soft sand. He poked the sand with his feet as he walked. He saw that Rohit had stopped in front of him. When he reached him, he saw that there was a huge banyan tree, under which was a small grave covered with a green sheet. To Dushyant, the tree and the grave looked like they were a part of some other place, painted by someone in the middle of the forest.

'Unreal,' Dushyant said. Rohit was about to move forward when Dushyant stopped him and signalled him to see something. A deer stood behind the grave and was looking at both of them. Rohit was stunned. He had never seen a deer before.

'No, don't look at it like this,' Dushyant said, 'look indirectly or it'll run away.'

Both of them walked to the grave, trying to not look the deer in the eye. The deer was alert, but it didn't run.

'People have a lot of faith in this dargah,' Rohit said and lay down on the dargah's plinth. Dushyant stood at the ground admiring the beauty. Rohit, still lying on the plinth, pulled Dushyant towards him. He stopped right before their lips could touch.

'What happened?' Dushyant whispered.

'I'm waiting for the flowers,' he said.

'Is it the end?' Dushyant asked, 'we've come far away. Don't stop now, don't say you're tired. Say you're looking for shade in the hot sun. We're stuck at that point in the story, where the vacant spaces of our lives are filled with sunlight. Now I've got a broom in my hand. You find a banyan tree in your pursuit of shade and listen to my anecdotes of cleaning for hours. I'm leaving tomorrow and our story ends here, at this dargah, under this banyan tree.'

'I wish I had my diary with me, I would have written it down.'

'Don't write everything down, leave something for living as well,' said Dushyant. He came close to Rohit.

'But this was poetry.'

'I said what I saw. What can you see?'

Rohit could feel Dushyant's breath on his lips.

'Why does pleasure taste so bitter when we experience it? And why does it drip like honey once it's gone?' he asked.

Rohit's body had surrendered. He saw sunflowers peeking out of Dushyant's eyes. Their petals fell on his lips. Slowly, he started to collect them from his lips.

'First I want to hear the rest of that poem.'

'Which poem?'

'The two lines you just said.'

'I've just started living it.'

'When can I hear it?'

'If you come to the roof alone tonight, I'll tell you the rest.'

Dushyant jumped up to the plinth and sat down near Rohit.

'There's friction between restriction and freedom in your writing,' said Dushyant.

'Is that so?' asked Rohit flirtatiously.

'You should write more. There's something waiting to burst inside you. Soon your books will be published, and everyone will get to read your work.'

'But I only write for you.'

'That's the beauty of your writing. It's both personal and universal at the same time. You'll write a lot more.'

'I'll not write a single word.'

Annoyed, Rohit went and lay down on the other side of the grave. Dushyant followed him and lay down near him. He was looking at the banyan tree.

'It's such a beautiful place. Why are there green threads hanging from this tree?'

'I don't know.'

Dushyant jumped and pulled a long green thread from the tree.

'Give me your hand,' he said.

'No, I don't want to give you anything.'

Dushyant sat on Rohit's stomach, held his hands and kissed them.

'Can I tie this thread on your hand?'

'Okay, tie it.'

'Are you sure? You'll be bound then?'

Rohit saw bunches of flowers on Dushyant's lips. He tried to get up to kiss them, but Dushyant pushed him down. He held his wrist and started to tie the thread on it. Something moved in the trees. They saw that the deer had come closer now. Dushyant kissed the thread on his wrist while looking at the deer.

'This is for our friendship.'

Rohit tied the remaining thread on Dushyant's wrist.

'We should take one for your Madam as well, she would like it,' Dushyant said and broke another thread off of the tree. Tying it around his finger he said, 'Shall we go?' He extended his hand towards Rohit to help him up. Rohit held his hand and pulled him close.

'I'm hungry for the flowers. Let me have my fill,' he said and started kissing Dushyant. At first, Dushyant couldn't hear the music Rohit was dancing to. Then Dushyant's body loosened up a bit, his mind started to focus, breaking all the connections with worries on the other side of the river and he started listening to Rohit's heartbeats, which were increasing by the minute. The deer moved away from the trees and came to stand near them. Both of them were moving to the same beat now and amidst all this, they would sometimes look over at the deer as though he was the only witness to this madness. Their naked bodies were covered in the mud from the dargah. Both of them were completely immersed in a dance whose music resonated everywhere around them. When at last they parted out of exhaustion, the deer bounded away inside the jungle, as though it had never been there.

Dushyant stood at the riverbank waving at Verma Madam. He could see that she too was waving back. Rohit suddenly remembered that they were supposed to take a watermelon back but by then Dushyant had run ahead and jumped in the water. Rohit jumped in after him. After a few strokes, Rohit realized that he was already tired from the journey there. His whole body ached. He wasn't used to this much swimming. When he stopped and looked over at Dushyant, he saw that he was swimming rapidly. He wanted to tell Dushyant to go slowly and take breaks, but he knew that Dushyant wanted to reach Verma Madam as soon as possible. Suddenly, Dushyant stopped in the middle of the river. Rohit was right behind him and stopped as well.

'What happened?' asked Rohit

'My shins are cramping up.'

Dushyant was in pain; Rohit could see it in his eyes.

'Don't kick as much and try relying more on your arms. And go slowly . . . you're swimming too fast, do it slowly, we're almost there.'

After a few breaths, they decided to resume swimming, but Dushyant kept stopping. Rohit realized that Dushyant was unable to bear the pain anymore. His face was red, and his eyes were bloodshot. Rohit held Dushyant's hand and said, 'Hold onto my shoulders. I'll pull you to the shore, just keep breathing.'

Dushyant held onto Rohit's shoulders tight. Rohit was having difficulty swimming, but he constantly communicated with Rohit.

'You don't have to do anything. Just don't let go. I'll keep swimming slowly.'

Rohit saw that Dushyant kept trying to reach down and touch his legs, which were cramping. Rohit knew how painful that could be. He began to feel anxious and swam more quickly. Every few strokes Dushyant's hands would slip off his shoulders, and Rohit would pull him back onto his shoulders again.

'Talk to me and keep your head above the water. Don't swallow the water or you'll become heavier.'

Rohit kept telling Dushyant what to do to stay afloat. Dushyant was staring at the sky. He was trying to breathe as much as he could. Every few minutes, Rohit heard Dushyant scream. He would stop for a minute and then resume swimming.

'We're almost there. Look at Verma Madam. Look, look.'

Dushyant moved his head up a little to look at her and his hand slipped off Rohit's shoulder. Rohit pulled his hand and put it around his neck. In a bid to breathe, Dushyant had now climbed on top of Rohit. Rohit realized that Dushyant's body was going stiff.

'Dushyant . . . see, we're almost here.'

He could hear Verma Madam's voice from the other side. She could see Dushyant hanging from Rohit's back. She was shouting Dushyant's name. Dushyant's attempts to breathe were applying pressure to Rohit's neck, making it difficult for him to breathe. By then they had almost reached Verma Madam. Rohit choked up and started to cough. He needed to breathe. Dushyant's weight was pulling him under water. They were just ten laps away from Verma Madam. To cough and breathe better, Rohit pulled away from Dushyant, but he couldn't stop coughing. Rohit moved his hands around and reached the riverbank. He was coughing violently now. That's when he heard Verma Madam's screams. When he looked back, he couldn't see Dushyant where he was supposed to be; instead, there were bubbles in the water nearby. His coughing hadn't ceased yet, but he jumped inside the river and dove deep where he saw the bubbles. Hearing Verma Madam scream, a crowd had gathered there. Rohit could see Dushyant's body deep under the water. His eyes were bulging. Rohit was surprised to see that his eyes weren't red but white. He was still having difficulty breathing, but he couldn't look away from Dushyant's eyes. He came back up to breathe and after a few deep breaths, went back under to pull Dushyant up, but his body had drifted further away. He swam deeper. Far down, behind a rock, he saw Dushyant's hand, a green thread tied to his finger, the thread he had wanted to give to Verma Madam. He held Dushyant's hand and tried to pull him up, but his body had become unbearably heavy. He swam near Dushyant and when he saw his frozen face, he started shaking him. He wanted to shout at him and ask him how he could lie there like a terrifying statue.

Rohit needed to breathe again. He started to swim upwards. But he couldn't leave Dushyant there like that. He wrapped his legs around Dushyant's torso and his hands around his neck. By then, many people had jumped into the water as well, where they found the two of them stuck to each other. It took a long time to separate them after they were pulled from the river. Both of their bodies had gone stiff. Verma Madam had lost her voice screaming. Tears streamed down her face and all sound seemed to drown in silence. She couldn't hear anything anyone said to her. She wanted to close her eyes and go to sleep right then and there, so when she opened her eyes, this all could be over like a bad dream. She closed her eyes, but Dushyant didn't come to her in her dreams.

I stopped writing and fell on the sofa, as though I'd been running for hours. I realized my face was wet, my eyes burned, and I was having difficulty breathing. I wanted to close my eyes, but I was afraid of what I might see when I did, so I didn't close them. But even with open eyes, I wasn't spared. I could see Dushyant's stiff body spread-eagled on the ceiling of my room. Verma Madam touched my hair and started caressing my head. I breathed a sigh of relief and closed my eyes.

'This is what I didn't want to write,' I said.

'What was it that you wanted to write then?'

'I just wanted to write a small story about love between a student and a teacher.'

'I too came to hear such a story, but then you brought in Dushyant. His name wasn't even Dushyant.'

'Yes, his name . . .'

'Now you can't even bring yourself to say the name "Pawan". You thought you would call him Dushyant and escape by telling a light and simple love story from the sidelines.'

'What a beautiful name. Pawan.'

I opened my eyes and spoke the name over and over. I saw the deer from the dargah standing on my ceiling.

I got up and went to the kitchen. I needed another glass of wine. But something happened once I reached the kitchen, and instead of the wine my hands opened the refrigerator and reached for the milk and ginger. I was involuntarily making tea. I was flummoxed: I could no longer control my characters or my hands. My heart desired a glass of wine, but my hands kept preparing tea. After some time, I came back to my computer with a cup of tea. As I looked at my story, it felt like I was standing alone at the peak of a high mountain. I didn't even want to climb the mountain. I wanted to limit the story to the valleys, where the pitfalls are small and only end in laughter. Even if you're the one who starts a story, midway through, the characters take the reins away. But once you reach the end, everyone disappears, and you're left standing alone. Now you're alone at the top of this mountain and you can see the story ending in the valley below and that's when you pray for one last push.

A hand with a green thread tied on its wrist gives me a light push and I start to fall in the end.

31

Rohit saw a lizard crawling on the roof of his room in the hospital. He asked the nurse to scare it away.

'This is an ICU. Lizards can't enter here.'

Whenever he complained to someone about the lizard in the room, they would just stare at him. Ma would cry. He couldn't understand why the mention of the lizard troubled everyone. He started to hide the fact that he could see the lizard. If the lizard came too close to him, he would shoo it away. But only when nobody was watching.

When he came back home, he was unable to tell anyone that the lizard from the ICU had somehow found its way to his room. He didn't know how. Whenever he dreamt of the river and being underwater, he would wake up and look for the lizard. During sleepless nights, the lizards would come close and play with his fingers. He didn't take his hand away. The same lizard that

made him scream bloody murder in the hospital now
lived with him.

Every morning I find your hair on the pillow next to me,
The stream of my dreams has dried, you and I run in its
bed
I couldn't tell you,
You were the answer to the riddle that I am
That I was the crazed deer and you were the musk
You never left
You never came
You were a stringless kite
I was a wet and entangled thread
I could never tell you
When joy comes to us
It tastes bitter and hard
Once it's gone, it drips like honey
I could never tell you
But I wanted to look beautiful to you
I wanted to climb inside your clothes and be you
I could never tell you
That I dressed your naked words with the garb of my lies
That I recited to you
What was already yours, just newly attired
You said it's poetry
I was a thief and you were the gold
I could never steal you
But whenever the prickle of your moustache
Reached from your lips to my stomach
Your smell emanated from the deer that I was.

Rohit touched the green thread tied to his wrist and instantly hated what he had written. He tore up the page. He needed to see Verma Madam. Only Verma Madam could understand his relationship with Dushyant. It had been so long, but it felt like it had only been yesterday that he had been swimming in the river. The mere thought of going up to the roof made him break out in a sweat. He kept waiting to gather courage and the days kept passing. He only learned what was happening outside by listening to the conversations in his house. He heard that Verma Madam was leaving the village. He wanted to meet her at least once before she left but couldn't gather the courage to face her. His mistake was beyond forgiveness or apology.

The grief we sense when somebody dies feels like the anguish of being cheated. We call out, but there's nobody to hear us on the other side. How can somebody just leave like that, in the middle of the conversation? Now he has left and taken his portion of the story with him and we're trying futilely to collect the scraps of our story in what remains of the tale.

One Sunday afternoon he untied the green thread from his wrist and put it in an envelope. He jumped from his terrace to Verma Madam's and then went downstairs to her house. The door to her room was closed. He slid the envelope under the door. For a while he stared at the corner of the envelope that peeped outside, waiting for it to be pulled in. He was about to leave when he heard some movement within. He couldn't stop himself now.

'Verma Madam, I just want to tell you that . . . Dushyant . . .' When he said his name he realized that he had no right to. Especially not in front of her. He cleared his throat.

'He went to the dargah on the far side of the river so that he could bring the sacred thread for you. This envelope has the green thread, and you . . .'

Rohit started stammering and the words stopped inside him. Guilt, bitterness, repentance, hatred and many other emotions wouldn't let him move away from the door. Even when he returned home, he felt like he still stood before the door, staring at the corner of the envelope.

The next day a tonga was waiting outside Verma Madam's house. She locked her door and stepped into the tonga, all the while her eyes scanning the ground. Rohit stood at the door to his house and watched her. Only when the tonga started to move did she look up at Rohit. Rohit saw in her eyes the lingering hope that Rohit might still dive in and save Dushyant. Verma Madam didn't take her eyes off his face, searching for an answer he didn't have. He saw that the green thread was tied to her wrist. Before he could look at her again, the tonga turned and disappeared from view.

We completely turn ourselves into the person we love. Their language, their laughter, their demeanour and their subtle movements, all start showing up in our daily life. We have no idea how and when they entered us, nor can we explain it. But when we see bits of them in us, we feel a pang of helplessness. We take a deep breath and unsuccessfully try to tuck those bits away.

Becoming someone or making someone your own is so like death!

  Does every riverbank story end with a drowning? Is it not possible to reach the other side without drowning? We keep collecting questions throughout life. You find answers for some of these, and some questions just fade away, but some stay with you your whole life in all their intensity. He hadn't been able to fulfil the promise that he'd one day meet Verma Madam. Even after he was gone, so much of Dushyant remained behind.

I finished the story, stood up and went to my bookshelf. I pulled out Camus' *The Outsider* from behind the other books. Months after leaving the village, Verma Madam had written to him for the first and last time. He had kept the letter safe in this book since then. I know the story would have had a better ending if I had included that letter in it, but some things are not to be put out into the world, so I hadn't. There are some true strands of the story that should remain out. The minute I opened the letter, a whiff of cinnamon flew up from the yellowed pages. The letter had kept the fragrance safe for so long. The more I hid this letter, the more I saw it everywhere.

  'Rohit,

  This Borges poem was one of Dushyant's favourites. He wanted to share it with you, so I am sending it to you:

> *You Learn*
> *After a while you learn the subtle difference*
> *Between holding a hand and chaining a soul,*

And you learn that love doesn't mean leaning
And company doesn't mean security . . .*

Forgive yourself if possible.

In memory of Pawan,

Antima Verma . . .'

I read the poem many times. I could still hear the timbre
of Dushyant's (or Pawan's) voice in my head. I put the
letter safely back in the book. That's when I saw the thread
peeking out from a corner of the book. I opened it again
and found that I had kept Dushyant's thread in the book
as well. I wanted to go back to the story and edit out the
part where I had written that I gave the thread to Verma
Madam. In reality, I had never given her the thread. I could
never gather the courage to face her. I was a coward and my
cowardice had stopped me. Actually, it wasn't cowardice, it
was the dishonesty of my survival. I wanted to escape. We
always want to escape even those allegations we know we'll
never have to face. I was surprised; Verma Madam was beside
me, but she still didn't stop me. Maybe your characters too
overlook some of your weaknesses and forgive you for your
helplessness. I put the book back and instantly sent the story
to my publisher.

---

* Jorge Luis Borges, 'After a While', revised and copyrighted by
Veronica Shoffstall.

32

Even when you find yourself completely spent, there's still something left. And in that leftover, you can travel to unlimited possibilities, rest at innumerable turns in the road and venture out to dense forests. Because of this pandemic, I couldn't go to any mountains or travel anywhere. I just roamed around my house in circles and recorded everything I did. Now I realize how important it was for everything outside to shut down . . . otherwise, I wouldn't have been able to look inside myself like this. I wouldn't have been able to find Dushyant in Pawan or hide Pawan in Dushyant. In reality, I was hiding underwater and whenever I looked up, I saw Antima Verma Madam standing on the surface of the river. And because there were ripples in the water, I saw multiple Antimas every time I looked up. I wanted to write about all the possibilities of Antima. And not just Antima Verma Madam, but her fragrance too; whenever I smelled it, I found her standing there.

It had been many days since I'd sent the story to my editor. I thought that maybe he didn't like it. I often wanted to call him and ask if he read it. But I couldn't bring myself to. My house felt the absence of Antima Verma Madam. My steps echoed in my house. Every step I took had lost its reason to reach anywhere. The story ends, and it takes away all the music of your being, but still, you keep trying to dance on in your stubbornness. Can't we save some music for ourselves? Just enough for us to rest our heads. Then the old woman whom I had seen sitting on the park bench started to take up residence in my mind. When I was thinking about her, a light tune emerged from somewhere and reached my ears. I closed my eyes and started to enjoy the music, and then I saw a banyan tree grow in the middle of a desert. Now my steps had a place to reach, a direction. I wanted to meet her right then. I wanted to rest under that banyan tree.

She was sitting on the bench in the park as if waiting for me. When I looked at her, I felt I had known her for ages. How had I passed her by all these days? What could her name be? When I went near her, I saw that there was a dead lizard in her lap. She looked at me like a child who had mistakenly broken her favourite toy.

'What happened?' I asked.

'I don't know . . . when I came here, I found her dead. There were ants all over her, so I cleaned her. I thought if I removed the ants, she might come alive.'

I sat beside her. Soon after, she picked up some dried leaves, wrapped the lizard in them and placed it in her small purse.

'I'll bury her in the *tulsi* at my home. When people die young, they need a quieter resting place.'

A while later the pain of the lizard's death had left her face. How old must she be? She must have seen many people pass away. Maybe after a certain age, death becomes an everyday occurrence; a minor irritant, like when the milk boils over on the stove. Is that why I want to grow old, so that I too can bury the people gone from my life too soon in quieter places?

'How old are you?' she asked me.

'I was just wondering about your age.'

'So . . .'

'Oh . . . I will turn forty-five soon.'

'You have lots of time.'

'At every age one feels they are very old.'

She laughed at this. Her laughter had so much joy I almost felt jealous.

'You know what old age is?' she asked. 'Being old is like being that guest in the wedding who should have left long ago after everything was done. But he's still there in the house, years after the wedding. That's why if someone blesses you with a long life, make them take it back. They actually want to exact revenge on you.'

There was joy in what she said. There's no better person than one who can laugh at themselves and their situation.

'What's your name?'

'Surbhi,' she said.

'That's why your eyes are so different from your face.'

She was embarrassed to hear that. Surbhi means deer. Am I on to my next story or am I still revolving around the first one?

'Is it okay if I call you Surbhi?'

'Are you falling in love with me?' she asked and started laughing. Watching her easy laughter, I laughed too. That's when my editor called.

'I'll have to take this call,' I said.

I got up from the bench and answered the call as I walked towards the banyan tree.

'Hello . . . yes?'

'I just finished reading the story. It's different now. When did Aru, father, Salim and Pawan join in? When I read it the last time it was just about Dushyant, Rohit and Verma Madam.'

That's when I realized my mistake.

'Oh! I have mistakenly sent you the process along with the story. It's a bad habit of mine. I write the process alongside the story. You let it be, just focus on the story.'

'No, no,' he interrupted me, 'I think this is more interesting.'

'What do you mean?'

'It's new for the process of writing to be published alongside the story itself.'

'But I've written so much in the process, I don't even remember.'

'It's not a story anymore.'

'Then?'

'It's a novel now. I'm stopping the print of the story collection and pushing this out first.'

'It's a novel?' I asked with surprise. 'I always thought that I would only write a novel when I was old.'

'Maybe you're old now,' he said and then laughed at his own joke. I don't remember what we talked about after that. I was looking at Surbhi now.

'It's good that you're here with me,' I said as I sat down near her again. 'I'm not alone.'

'You look happy.'

'I wrote my first novel without meaning to.'

'You're a writer?'

'Yes.'

'Then read me something.'

Although I generally get irked by such requests, there was such innocence in her demand that I laughed.

'I've written a poem after ages . . . actually that's why I wanted to meet you today. To read this poem to you.'

'Then let's hear it.'

She looked at me like a newborn baby looks at the world.

Like a tangled and old piece of string,
She sits on the park bench, bunched up in herself,
Taking as little space as possible,
Keeping the whole universe inside her.
Her smile doesn't reach her eyes.
Can I touch her?
Can you stare deep into the crevices on her face?
She doesn't need anybody.
Then why does a leaf fly in and rest in her lap?
Why does a lizard bear witness to her existence?
I see a poem about a lizard sitting on a dry leaf,
Whom she is keeping alive inside her like a banyan tree.

I finished reading the poem and she placed her hand on my shoulder. She was sad.

'I wish the lizard could have listened to this beautiful poem too.'

The death of the lizard had changed the meaning of the poem. I took her hand in mine and realized that all of my ideas of softness had been wrong. Her hands were soft. She was staring at the banyan in front of her.

'When you sit in front of banyan and peepal trees in cities, it gives you the illusion of being in the mountains,' she said.

'Is that why you sit here?'

'I sit here for no reason, but reasons emerge as I sit.'

'I find trees fickle. They don't have the patience of mountains in them.'

'You're a writer; why don't you live in the mountains?'

'I don't know the answer to that question. If I try to find a reason, I can only say that you need cities to write about the mountains and you have to go to the mountains to write about the cities.'

'What irony!'

'Where were you born?'

She took a pen and a diary from her purse and started writing in it. She was writing, not saying anything but I could still hear it.

'I was born in Lahore. Don't ask the year. The years didn't mean anything then. When I was little, I wanted to turn into a butterfly but didn't want to undergo the pain of metamorphosis. Can we ever save ourselves from anything?'

My novel was fading away and Surbhi was a butterfly flying out of the mist. As though a deer had found beautiful wings.

Covid-19 had slowly lost its intensity. The deaths, news of the deaths and fear of the deaths had all gone away. At first, doctors were testing medicines, but now they trusted some. India was still at number two in the world with the number of cases, but everyone was slowly returning to work. Pfizer and BioNTech had announced that they had found vaccines for the virus. According to their tests, the vaccines had a 90 per cent success rate in saving people. There were some other companies as well who claimed to be in the third round of testing. The whole world saw a vaccine for the virus at the next turn. Even if the vaccine was created early, it would still take time to reach everyone. The virus had been present long enough that people had devised clever ways to live with it. Sometimes, I felt that because we had watched so many films about the end of the world, we all had imagined a day where we too would be a part of such a film. And then the virus came and so arrived the day for us to be a part of that film. But nobody knew that the movie would last so long. We'd been living inside an extremely boring film for months now. Neither we nor our governments had any idea about the plot of this slog-fest of a movie. Because of our habit of waiting for magic, the biggest roles were taken up by the religious gurus, market and leaders. Whereas the main roles in this film should have gone to the scientists. But such instances for profit come once in a lifetime. Who would let it go? The rest of the people had put masks over their eyes, rather than their mouths, and after drawing a deep breath of this new normal, they had stepped out of their houses to play the roles of supporting characters in the film. Not that they saw any other options in front of them. In this never-ending film, everyone is alone and responsible for their own life.

I entered my empty home with Surbhi accompanying me. I could see her story in every crevice of the house. Lahore was in the kitchen. The outer room was Punjab and in the bedroom, she was settling down in Bombay. I was pacing around between Lahore, Punjab and Bombay. I wasn't the same Rohit who stood on his terrace with the wet and tangled string. I had changed. I was trying to find ways to enter Lahore via Punjab. In this pursuit, the butterfly of a tiny joy started to fly around on my balcony. And to experience that joy I turned my computer on and wrote:

'Long ago, a girl named Surbhi lived in Lahore, who wished to turn into a butterfly.'

THE END

Translator's Acknowledgements

I'm grateful to Manav Kaul for giving me the opportunity to translate his debut novel. Thanks to my publisher, Vaishali Mathur at Penguin Random House, for giving this translation a home and entertaining my endless questions, and to Yash Daiv for editing this manuscript. I'm deeply grateful to Rebecca DeWald, Victoria Maitland and everyone at the National Centre for Writing for the best mentorship opportunity ever. Thank you, Vineet Lal, for conceptualizing and funding the NCW Saroj Lal Mentorship. I couldn't be more thankful for this wonderful chance of a lifetime. I would like to thank my mentor, friend and translator extraordinaire, Daisy Rockwell, without whom none of this would have been possible. Thanks for your generosity and confidence in me, and for letting me use your translation of Sarveshwar Dayal Saxena's poem 'Tumhare Saath Rehkar' in this book. I'm grateful to Kanishka Gupta, the best agent ever, for taking me under his wing and for always being there to answer my questions: your dedication to translated literature is unparalleled. Thanks to my translator friends, Akshaj Awashthi, Aratrika Dasgupta, Kartikeya Jain and Shivangi Pandey. Thank you, Rutba Shah, the translator who by her own admission will never translate again. Thank you, Ashwin Rajeev, my first reader and editor, for identifying the translator in a failed academic. Thank you for your love, care, support and, most importantly, for always listening to me. Thanks are due to my non-translation friends Avik Sarkar, Ashutosh Madhwani, Anjali Mittal, Ezrah, Jayasri, Niharika Aggarwal, Rishabh Shukla, Ritika Goel, Swastika Mittal, Ujjwal Jain, Vani Khokar, Wesley D'Souza, and many more who lent a friendly ear along the way. Last, but definitely not least, I'm grateful to my family. To my parents, Pankaj Sharma and Sudha Shukla, who are uncertain about the career choice I've made, but support me, nonetheless. And to my brother, Uday Sharma, for teaching me market appeal and helping with random words at ungodly hours.

Scan QR code to access the
Penguin Random House India website